Praise for Opus 1

"If you're a D&D fan you will love this book a LOT too. Things will feel so familiar yet so different at the same time."
   - DW

"This book was difficult to put down! There were so many twists, and the story was so beautifully written and so descriptive that I could see every scene and character so clearly in my mind."
   - DS

"The Ballad of the Emerald Bard: Opus 01 is a beautifully written fantasy full of emotion, mystery, and depth. El'Mindeeya Do'Katal is a compelling character, and each story reveals new layers of her world and her heart. Powerful, poetic, and unforgettable."
   - SB

"This is not a book for those looking for a straightforward fantasy adventure. It's a slow burn, character-driven, and introspective collection that demands emotional engagement. But for readers who want depth, musical metaphor, and a heroine who will linger in your thoughts long after the final stanza The Ballad of the Emerald Bard Opus 01 is a rare gem."
   - LF

The Ballad of the Emerald Bard

Also by Dan Bonser

Ballad of the Emerald Bard
Opus 02 – The Suite of Wolves, Poison and Revelry

The Ballad of the Emerald Bard

Opus 01

The Suite of Seduction, Lost Love, and Revenge

By Dan Bonser

Illustrations by DKYingst and Tarah (Condell) Hardy

Cover by Eddy-Shinjuku

The Ballad of the Emerald Bard – Opus 01 – The Suite of Seduction, Lost Love, and Revenge
The Nocturne of the Deal at the Crossroads
A Symphony of Old Debts
The Sonata of Buried Secrets

First Printing: 2016/03/20

Fifth Edition

© 2016, 2026 Dan Bonser. All rights reserved.
Published by Lawson-Bonser Publishing

ISBN-13: 979-8-9930052-0-1

Cover design by Eddy-Shinjuku on DeviantArt and Dan Bonser
https://www.artstation.com/eddy-shinjuku

Interior character illustrations by DKYingst on Deviant Art and Dan Bonser
http://www.deviantart.com/art/Comm-Madrin-384609389

Treble/Base Clef Heart Illustration, Sonnetic Axe and Elven Kukri, and Interior character Illustrations by Tarah (Condell) Hardy
https://tarah6692.artstation.com/projects/85dZ6

Content Note

This book contains mature and disturbing themes, including sexual violence, demonic assault, predatory behavior, and scenes involving giant spiders.

Additional content includes explicit sexual content, violence, trauma, and emotional distress.

Reader discretion is advised.

Acknowledgments

To all my friends and family, who always believed I had a talent, no matter how long it took to actually manifest into something worthwhile.

To El'Mindeeya Do'Katal, for coming into my life when I needed her the most, and staying with me, long after her first story ever ended and mine had long since moved on.

But mostly, mainly, to my wife, who inspires me just by breathing, for coming into my life, and pushing me to be the man everyone knew I could become.

The Orchestration of Opus 01

Foreword and Definitions

Nocturne, Symphony, and Sonata – These are defined as "complete" compositions or pieces of work.

Movements – These are defined as "Self-Contained Parts" of musical compositions, or, as used within, Chapters.

Opus – Traditionally defined as a collection of compositions, ofttimes, but not always, following a theme.

All compositions contained within are, in their own rights, full, self-contained short stories, although they have been tied together by the threads of an overarching plotline moving the story forward. So, in that way, they are one consistent timeline and are meant to be read in order.

1: The Nocturne of the Deal at the Crossroads

Movement 1: A Bard on the Stage

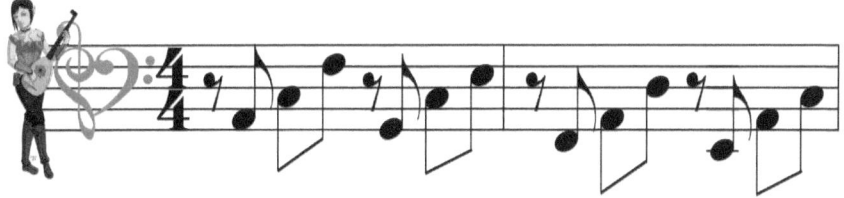

An alluring song drifted in the air, like a fine mist of melody. It did not need the words that were floating along with the chords emanating from the lute, yet they were there. Altogether, the music was beautiful, yet moody. Melancholy, if a single word could be used to describe such emotional music as it landed upon the audience's ears like newly made snowflakes. It was a simple song, as the best often were. A simple song about lost love. Mournful, moving, a risky song for a stage in a dark inn at the crossroads in a deep, dark, deadly forest, where shadows prey upon weary travelers simply seeking refuge from the dark elements. The short, dark-haired bard moved her hands smoothly around her lute and lightly upon the strings with the skill of someone who had handled the instrument for a lifetime. Some of the words spoke of her past, a past of pain and sorrow. It was a song that spoke of matters of the heart.

Some days, without you, are exactly the same
Some days are quite mundane

Some days I wake up crying
Believing that to myself, I am lying

Lying about you being gone
Lying about our love gone wrong

The bard's costume clung to her like mist, revealing more skin than it concealed. It was crafted to catch the audience's eye and hold them captive. Designed in two sections, the halter top was a lattice of silk and gold thread patterning, accentuated with green emeralds. The fabric cradled her chest, shaping a graceful décolletage. The straps that wrapped her neck were decorated with faux green feathers that lay across her shoulders. From the sides of her top, sheer fabric hung down over her rib cage like curtains. The top left her upper chest and belly bare, revealing her skin, which held an ethereal, almost inhuman quality. A large, emerald teardrop, the size of her thumb's first knuckle, hung from a black choker accentuated with tiny white wolves. The gem rested gently in the small notch between her collarbones, catching the light with her every breath.

The chords her deft fingers coaxed from the lute matched her melodic voice in an oddly haunting way, almost as if a magic spell was being cast upon the notes that hung in the air. The lyrics themselves continued with their anguish.

Some of these days I can block it all out
Some days, I fall to my knees and shout

Screaming my needs into the night
But, of course, only the willow-wisps hear my plight

Tonight, I sing this song for you
Kissed with the dreams I shared with you.

From her waist down she wore an intricate skirt, consisting of two sections. It split into flowing panels of sheer green fabric, leaving the front and sides of her legs completely bare, a deliberate design, allowing freedom to move and dance. Centered upon the front panel was an emblem, a treble clef entwined with a bass clef, their curves forming into the romantically stylized shape of a heart. The back, or skirt, section had a detailed array of patterns that were as plainly elven as her pointed ears: trees, nature, that magic and miracle of life, all shown through designs of dark emerald with gold embroidery. Overall, the sheer, lightweight fabric started at her waist with the same light green as her top which faded into a far darker, emerald green at the bottom.

The song's remorseful tone seemed to infect everyone in the room. It might have been a seedy place to be, but this inn was built at a major crossroads of the world. All sorts of folks stopped here, and on this night, the main tavern hall was filled. As the song went on, some folks thought of lost loves. Some thought about their families which were much further down the road. No matter what the song itself brought out of the minds of the patrons, it touched everyone in the room in some way, for even the hardest adventurer had loved someone, once upon a time.

That was no easy task, I can assure you
To move me so much, to raise you above the few

The elven bard wore little else of note upon the stage. On her side was her single weapon, a small tomahawk-like axe with a blade that was smithed into the same emblem that was emblazoned on the front section of her skirt. The silvery blade caught the light at times, giving it an almost magical shimmer that made it seem, to the casual observer, more ornamental than functional. She had on green enameled vambraces that seemed the most out of place of the entire wardrobe. They covered her entire forearms, yet she wore them like a second skin. If one looked closely, they seemed to have oddly designed lines all over them. Her feet were encased within slipper-like shoes that had, what seemed to be, a single strap that wound around her well-formed calf muscles like the vines that adorned her top.

Her skin held a muted warmth, lighter than her woodland kin but deeper than the pale city elves. A subtle mark of a childhood spent away from the ancient forests, in places where even the sun could not grant the blessings only deep roots could give.

The bard's fingers breathed one final chord into the air in an almost magical, enchanted way. Her voice lingered behind, singing the final lyrics:

So, on this night, please don't let me be a shrew
When I say, "I have loved." I only think of you.

She sang the last five words, in almost a whisper, holding the "you" for an extended time, letting it fade away with the final chord from the lute. It had been a beautifully vivid song about lost love. It was an odd tactic, ending a concert on a truly sad song, yet obviously a smart choice as the song was haunting, and oft times, leaving an audience haunted would keep the bard's song inside their head for some time after.

As her final note faded into silence, she opened her eyes and truly looked at the crowd for the first time since she had begun the song. There was a lingering moment of bated breath, and within that moment she spotted a man, a hardened adventurer dressed in scarred leather at the bar, gently wiping a tear from his eye. As he flung it aside, he started the applause that quickly enveloped the room. The female elf bowed deeply. Being a bard was normally a thankless business, especially being a female elf. One would go from town to town and simply play background music at some wayward tavern for not very much. Sure, some folks would pay attention, but most of the time when they did pay attention, she noticed, it was more at her appearance than her music. This inn, The Darkened Deal, was different on this night. It was different for one reason and one reason only. The owner.

The applause, which hung in the air throughout the room, brought a smile to the bard's face. It had been a sad love song, almost bringing tears to her own dark green, elven eyes. Her short, boyish, black hair framed her elven face, bringing out her eyes, in a very feminine way. If she were human, one would suggest that she was in her mid-twenties, but considering she was an elf, there was no way to tell how old she could possibly be, as her species was eternal.

Her voice held a magical quality and her melodies had a way of weaving around the soul with a will of their own. Most who ever got to be around her for any length of time knew there was a far deeper mystery to the bard than she would ever let on. Some few people had an inkling of her story, most never would. Yet above the bard and the crowd, on a catwalk lining the western wall of the Inn, stood the owner of the Darkened Deal. She was one of those few that believed she knew something about the bard's secrets. Ironically, her mind wondered, as she looked down upon the bard from above, how much the bard knew about the owner's own mysteries. If someone were to describe the owner as a "beautiful pirate-looking woman" they would not be wrong, but Tessa was so very much more deadly and erotic than simply beautiful.

On this night, Tessa wore a loose black shirt held together with loose laces, her voluptuous breasts, not restrained by anything, were teasingly on near full display. Her waist was cinched by belts, heavy with countless throwing daggers. Straps over her shoulders secured twin short swords to her back that were nearly hidden by a raven black mane of thick, curly hair. The shoulder straps, at times, seemed to be the only thing holding her loose shirt to her body, as the short sleeves fell off her shoulders, making them just long enough to reach her wrists. Her black leather pants were skin tight and often creaked when she walked. Tessa was obviously athletic, even though the many straps across her pants hid her musculature. She was a woman armed to the teeth and ready for anything. She had to be. The Deal at the Crossroads, or simply the Deal, as the regulars called the Darkened Deal, was an Inn in the middle of nowhere, and quite often frequented by the roughest folks to walk the long roads that crossed a short distance from the doors. She carried herself with a ruthless sensuality. Every glance, every pose, every breath was a calculated weapon. A femme fatale in every sense of the word.

The human-looking woman had many vices, simply because Tessa was a woman who indulged. She removed the fragrant cigar from her mouth and clapped appreciatively along with her clientele. The final song the bard had finished singing had reminded her of so very much in her past, lost love, even the beauty of true love, but she pushed it all aside as she refused to be an emotional woman. She leaned over the railing of the catwalk, allowing gravity to test her top's bindings in a precarious way, above the main room as she said, "Bravo! Ladies and gentlemen, and whomever else may be around…." The smirk that followed the sarcastic comment led to many a laugh from the room below her. She continued on, "The Darkened Deal has been proud to present El'Mindeeya Do'Katal, the Emerald Bard!"

The Emerald Bard sat the lute she had been playing upon the stand next to her and bowed to the crowd, before bowing to the owner above her and to her right. Truly odd indeed. A wandering bard getting a standing ovation for a concert. El'Mindeeya Do'Katal, or Deeya as she was known to her friends, was very appreciative though, she soaked in the applause with a grateful smile. As she rose from the bow to the woman on the catwalk, she made sure to acknowledge the kiss and a wink Tessa launched in her direction by blowing a kiss back. Even though she knew the affection was just an act, Deeya knew how much appearances mattered…. Tessa had a reputation for "sharing her charms" with only those she considered to be the absolute best in what they did.

The concert was over and the patrons of the Deal went back to their drinking, gambling, and being an overall unsavory crowd. As Deeya packed up her stage equipment, including her lute, she could not help but be amazed at the establishment itself. The Inn stood at a major crossroads of the world. It was rugged country, not enough space for a city, but it was odd that it stood alone. The dark forest, which surrounded the Inn for miles in all directions, always had a menacing presence, and the forest itself sat in a valley surrounded by mountains. It was fascinating and eerie all at the same time. In all four directions lay many, many cities, yet there was nothing at all within half-a-day's travel in any of the four directions of intersection of the crossroads, nothing but river, rocks, (supposedly haunted) dark forest, and jagged, near impassable mountains. A major river ran behind the Deal and the inn itself maintained the two bridges close by, solidifying its importance and longevity. One could just pass the inn by in a day's hard march, if they went from one point of civilization to another, but for many the Darkened Deal was a welcome respite from the hard travel.

Deeya slung her pack on her shoulder, it held her sword and her lute with straps on the sides, her change of clothes, and everything she needed for her traveling life. She normally kept it with her, even if she had a room of her own. She took one last look at Tessa before she stepped off the stage. The exotic woman had descended the spiral stairs that landed on a raised area in the southwest corner of the great hall which held a single table. From that table, Tessa could sit and see, and be seen by, everyone in the establishment as it was across the room from the bar itself. Tessa currently reclined in her seat, with her booted feet up on the table, smoking her cigar while someone whispered in her ear. If this scene were anywhere else, such as a dark room, in a seedy tavern, at the end of a dark alley, in the roughest section of a big city, then Tessa would have fit perfectly into the role of the boss of a guild of thieves.

Deeya stepped off the stage, which was positioned against the north side of the room, and descended into the throng on the main floor of the building. The room itself was quite large with many tables, most of which were filled with members of merchant caravans or groups of adventurers. Deeya was not a large person, by any stretch of the imagination, normally not even coming up to people's shoulders, but the crowd parted widely for her. Many stopped and congratulated her on her performance, bringing up this song or that song, briefly telling how it affected them in some way. Deeya was used to being recognized, she had been a traveling bard for quite a long time, but this was a first, having so much trouble making it from one side of the room to another.

"I saw you in the capital years ago."

"My father told me about your voice healing him when he heard you sing after that one great war campaign."

"Your voice is enchanting, I didn't know bards could sound so pretty."

"I didn't even know you sang, I remember you once in a bar playing your lute."

"Emerald Bard, you have made my new favorite color green!"

"I never met an elf I liked, but you are an exception."

"I have to stop here twice a month on my routes and anyone Tessa approves of as much as you...well I'll be sure to spread the word about how great you are!"

Deeya took it all with a smile and a reply or comment. It never quite got as overwhelming as she would remember it being, though when she made it to the stairs at the southeast corner that led up to the rooms in the lodging wing, she sighed to herself. Freeing herself from the throng was quite liberating. Two flights of stairs got her to the second floor of rooms, which was the third floor of the Eastern Wing that stood over the stables. She yearned to get to her room and change into something comfortable. The flutter of her sectioned skirt around her bare legs distracted her. Upon opening the door she found a parchment that had been slid under it. She laid her pack gently on the soft bed and picked up the parchment, unfolded it, and read it.

I look forward to having your beautiful self join me briefly at my table before our talk later in my office.
Yours, Tessa

Deeya needed a drink, she confessed to herself. She had already planned to go back out to the bar, especially since she wanted to hear the other bards that Tessa had hired for ambiance music. Tessa had arranged this entire performance thing, so Deeya had known she was to pay her respects by returning. Tessa had not pulled all these strings for nothing, so this additional invitation was a bit much, but Deeya took it in stride. Tessa needed something, and Deeya thought about the name of the Inn, wondering if this was truly going to be a Darkened Deal at the Crossroads....

Tessa and Deeya had a long history, which was odd in and of itself. Deeya had seen so many Inns come and go, owners growing old before her eyes and retiring or passing on. But Tessa, Tessa remained the same, ageless. It had bothered Deeya for a decade or more, but Tessa was a friend with firm connections to the underbelly of the world, which was an asset. She locked the door and disrobed while she thought. She had taken a warm bath earlier, a luxury she enjoyed so very much that it was hard to keep her eyes from lingering lustfully upon the copper tub in the corner.... Not every room in the inn had a tub and Deeya normally never sprang for a suite such as this one, but Tessa had given her the room for this visit, however long it lasted, for free, due to the concert, and whatever else the woman had yet to ask of Deeya....

Tessa owned the Darkened Deal, for sure, but what kept the inn in business was not the clientele, or the bridges, it was Tessa's biggest "informal job." Tessa was an information broker. Every piece of gossip, every piece of news, came through this intersection before moving on to the big cities further onward down the roads. Tessa was in good with many bards, treating most of them like kings and queens, because bards were the best information finders there were. Welcomed into any inn, any gathering, any party, free to mingle with any crowd. It was hard not to overhear conversations told over a mug of ale. People liked sitting close to the bards sometimes, because their whispers would be drowned out by the music.

Those secrets sold to those like Tessa who then sold them to others. Deeya had other agendas with the information she often heard, but when she knew she was in possession of something lucrative to share, she knew Tessa was always buying.

Tessa had converted most of the inn itself into an information brokerage. The entire staff, from the bar wenches to the bartenders to those that cleaned the rooms, were the true inner workings. Patrons often did not even have to talk with Tessa directly. Ofttimes someone stealing a quick kiss or grope on a serving wench was actually nothing more than a bit of information entering or leaving Tessa's web.

Deeya had been at the Deal, already, for a night, and had slept well, so she was not yet tired, even though it was already quite late. She looked at her traveling clothes that she had laid out from her pack. Soft, comfortable, versatile, and modest. The bard never liked to "dress-up" as it were. She had met far too many a bard who enjoyed to dress quite immodestly.

Deeya had been on the road for some time, so she stretched in her nude skin for a moment before re-dressing herself. Her emerald teardrop that fell from her choker was cold in her clavicle. Her vambraces also stood out in stark green contrast to her not overly sun-darkened skin. For a moment she missed the solitude of her tree-top home in the elven city of Fo'Est, so very far away. But she stopped herself from falling into a reverie and got dressed, steeling herself for what was to come. It was time to get to work.

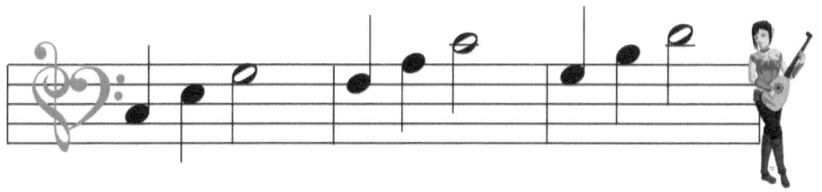

Movement 2: Into the Fray

She had been invited here by Tessa. The entire concert idea was Tessa's. She obviously wanted something from Deeya, though what it was, the bard had no clue. She slipped on her semi-tight-fitting dark brown leather pants and put on her belt. She attached all the extra straps that came along with the belt that she did not wear when on stage. Normally, she would wrap her chest with a long strip of cloth, to hold her breasts in place, but she chose to just pull on her loose, green cloth shirt. The shirt fell off her shoulders and left her upper chest and belly bare. She then put on her leather under-bust corset which had four leather cinching straps in the front, along with other straps that connected to her belt. The straps wrapped up around her shoulders and around her back. She put the axe in its holder on her right hip and sheathed her curved, elven kukri in one of the two scabbard-like things on her back. The other was for her lute, which she planned to leave behind. The corset and harness fit her well and gave her that sense of security she always enjoyed, as it meant she was armed and ready. She tugged her shirt into place, favoring modesty over spectacle. Deeya wasn't one to put her body on display, but strength, skill, and song had shaped her, and she wore them with quiet pride. Although distinctly feminine, Deeya had always held a boyish charm.

She slipped on her gloves that tucked into her vambraces and gave a final check to all her hidden weapons and gadgets before exiting the room. She shut the door behind her, but held on to the handle as she locked it. After she was done with the key, she put both hands on the handle and hummed softly for just a handful of seconds. It almost seemed as if the handle took on a glow…almost…. And if it did, it was only for a moment.

When she returned to the common room of the Darkened Deal, Deeya was shocked to see the crowd had slacked off quite a bit. There were still many patrons, but many tables were open, as were many spots at the long bar at the corner of the room to her right. Tessa was still reclining in her chair, although a table wench was leaning over Tessa's shoulder, whispering in her ear, allowing her ample cleavage to rest upon Tessa's shoulder. On the stage were a pair of male bards, both dressed rather drably. One played a harp, the other a lute. The tune that came from the duo was a nice lilting tune, one perfectly fit to be nothing more than background music. The song was calming and fun. A simple song that made one want to sit down and have a conversation over a stiff drink.

Deeya turned right after she exited the stairwell and walked to the bar to order an ale. The human tending the bar was one of the few male staff. Deeya had never been sure exactly how many staff there actually were, but it was more than obvious, after several visits to the Deal, that there were less men than women. And those women were all selected as much for their charm and sharp wits as their pleasant appearance. Beauty was as much a currency here as information, and both were traded with skill. Deeya knew all too well, if you were wanting information, nothing loosens men's lips more than the right woman.

The bartender slid Deeya her mug and said, "The Mistress is waiting for you to accompany her for a meal." Deeya could not help but feel Tessa's gaze brushing her back, unseen but palpable.

She visibly sighed and said, "I just needed a drink after singing. I won't be long."

He nodded, pulled out a rag, and started wiping down another part of the bar. Around her, Deeya listened to the talk. Some discussed her music, some discussed how a duke from a neighboring territory had taken on a sorceress as a mistress who was taking over the kingdom, and another pair of folks were discussing how a recent dwarven expedition had discovered a new gold vein near a town to the west. Deeya had heard most of the stories being told around her before and none of them particularly interested her. She made a mental note, though, not to head to the territory ran by Duke Quinlan within the kingdom ruled by the Kell monarchy. She had heard the story in a few other places, though she had heard that the sorceress was the Duke's mother,

sister, or lover, and either an elf or a human.
 Sorceresses, no matter who they were to anyone else,
were hardly ever worth tangling with.

 The ale did not last long in Deeya's hands. Being
an elf, she had a high tolerance to alcohol, yet she never
drank too much, even when she drank dark red wine.
Nothing ever quite helped the throat after singing like
ale, though. There were many facets to the Emerald
Bard, the elven side that liked forest and solitude, the
bardic side that liked inspiring and being inspired, and
the side of her that had been raised in a human society
which enjoyed laughing with friends. Then there was
the part of herself that was an odd mixture of all aspects
of her being which liked nothing more than the simple
pleasure of being alone for just a moment within a
crowded room. Above all, Deeya enjoyed the simplest of
pleasure.

 She knew that some people's simple pleasures were
different than her own and she found herself mentally
preparing for what was to come next. Outwardly,
though, she was trying to look exhausted even though
she was in no way tired. *Appearances*, she thought
sardonically, to herself…. She sat the empty mug upon
the bar, ran her fingers through her short hair, stood,
and made her way across the great hall to the corner
opposite the bar. As she reached the half-way point she
noticed that the bards on stage had finally noticed her,
because they started to play one of her own more
requested compositions. The words, which were not
being sung, were about an ancient town being attacked
by a dragon before a pair of heroes saved it. An ancient
tale of love and heroism in the face of the ultimate

destruction that comes with fire. It was a tale her dwarven friend's grandfather used to tell her. It was hard not to hum along to the song with a smile as she walked across the room.

Tessa's eyes drank in the Emerald Bard as Deeya ascended the steps to Tessa's raised private table. "Beautiful set, Bard."

Deeya smirked into Tessa's leering gaze and asked, "Are you talking about my performance tonight or...?" She leaned forward with a mischievous tilt of her head, flexing her shoulders forward, making her chest swell ever so slightly. Her smirk deepened into a bawdy grin as she slid into the seat beside Tessa, whose gaze was decidedly elsewhere. Deeya always hated oversexualization that so often came with being a bard, but she knew Tessa's game, and if there was one sure way to win, it was to play it even harder.

Tessa's deep blue gaze found Deeya's as she settled into the chair's embrace. She replied, "All of it," before she sucked in on her cigar and blew the fragrant smoke away from Deeya. It smelled of apples. Deeya would never smoke, as she knew how it would damage her voice, but the cigars that Tessa smoked had a uniquely enticing aroma. "You know, Bard, I would make you rich beyond belief if you'd sing a private song for me. Nude."

Deeya struggled not to roll her eyes. Tessa was quite the male when it came to propositions. She understood the allure of power and speaking powerful words. It worked for men who wanted to be with a powerful woman, and it worked for women who liked to melt under a strong woman's power. Sure, the bard struggled not to roll her eyes, but she could not help her body's response of being excited as well. "Only the tree that is my house gets that pleasure. A shame it doesn't pay."

Tessa smirked, flicking ash over a bucket that sat on the far side of her. "Oh, to be a tree...." She then leaned forward, the plunge of her neckline leaving little to the imagination. Deeya kept her green eyes stubbornly fixed on the woman's face, refusing to give her the satisfaction as Tessa used her husky voice to whisper, "If I were a man though...you'd turn part of me into a tree...."

Ah, the game.... Deeya took the opportunity to one up Tessa one last time by ending this round. She reached up and caressed the woman's cheek. A small gesture, but Deeya knew how the smallest of touches often meant so very much. Tessa visibly flinched at the touch. Tessa knew that she would never truly have Deeya, so she pushed the lewd game to extreme limits, so when Deeya added the slightest of intimate physical contact to the game, it caught Tessa off guard. The touch itself lingered as Deeya leaned forward and whispered into Tessa's ear. "Oh, my old friend, if you were a man, you would never get to feel this smallest touch of my skin, let alone see it."

After making sure that Tessa knew that she had inhaled the spicy scent of the woman's hair, Deeya leaned back into her chair. Her perfect timing paid off as the serving girl laid the platter of food in front of them. Most everyone knew that Deeya only loved women, but few knew why she'd never let a man touch her. She kept that secret locked away inside a journal she kept about that time, so very long ago, before she had become a mother, before she knew how violent a man could truly be.

Tessa leaned back as well, picking up a turkey leg and taking a bite. She was buying herself time to cool down. She had been confident she would always win the game, because she knew she would never actually have the bard, but by Deeya almost presenting the idea of even the slightest chance of victory...she had inspired Tessa to dream the impossible. Obviously, Tessa's imaginations of the passions the bard might possess had caused a spark within Tessa's loins that was not easy to extinguish.

Deeya took a fork and stabbed a small steak and then added some of the vegetables to it. The array of food, which had arrived on the platter, looked more like a buffet than anything else. One or two of everything the cooks at the inn made was represented, all piled into individual mounds of food. The near feast was far more than the two women at the table could eat, but Deeya knew that the display was more for showing off wealth and power. Incredibly rich merchants stopped here on the way between cities and Tessa never shied away from showing that she was an elite along with them.

Tessa finished chewing her turkey and said, "Thank you for coming, Deeya, you know I don't call in favors often."

Deeya swallowed her own mouthful of food and said, "Thank you for the concert. This kind of stunt will help get me more gigs in the neighboring lands."

Tessa shrugged while chewing her next bite. When she was done she put on a serious face. Her eyes seemed to avoid Deeya's own as Tessa said, "When we finish eating, you and I are going to retire to my suite, I'm going to close the curtains, and I'm going to ask you something I can ask no one else. If you agree you'll have to stay here for a few more days. If you do not, then you should probably stay anyways, you'll have a letter here soon."

Deeya knew not to ask about the business yet, but curiosity made her ask about, "A letter, you say?"

Tessa nodded, waving her bare turkey leg bone, "There has been a letter sent to you that has been following you for a small amount of time. While lingering here, it will find you."

Tessa tossed the bone into her ash bucket as Deeya contemplated the people that might be trying to contact her. While she sat and ate, a serving girl came up to share hushed words with Tessa. The serving girl had dark skin and straight dark hair. Slender and athletic, much the same build as Deeya, a uniquely beautiful woman. Even Deeya, with her elven hearing, could not make out what the words she whispered to Tessa were. Instead of trying to listen, Deeya studied the dark-skinned server with a practiced eye; poised, graceful, and clearly trusted enough to press her body against Tessa's to bring whispers to her ear.

The smoking room, in which the dark-skinned woman normally worked, was a room in the north wing of the Deal, which could be entered by a door beside the stage. The door itself led to a hallway where bouncers kept the typical rabble out of the exclusive, richer wing of the inn. The north wing was for guests who had too much money to find themselves mingling with those that frequented the main hall, which was more of a tavern setting. Hushed conversation and clandestine deals were to be had in the library's cushioned seats, or the small gambling room.

Deeya knew that from Tessa's suite you could see down into all of the major rooms that made up the common areas of the Darkened Deal, as well as out into the exquisite and tranquil gardens behind the inn. She had never been inside the suite itself, but she knew the glass that were the windows of the suite could be seen from almost any location. Though she had never seen Tessa "displayed" in them, she had seen a number of the staff, and even some clientele over the years, in all different degrees of immodesty before the curtains were drawn, if they eventually were.

Deeya reclined back into her chair, indicating she was done eating. Tessa said something about bringing a bottle of "the best" to the dark-skinned serving girl who bowed to Tessa and smiled at Deeya before she turned and walked back to the entrance to the smoking room. Tessa leered at her as she left. When Tessa returned her gaze to Deeya, her grin was representative of the thoughts running through her head. But instead of repeating those bawdy thoughts she said, "Chanti's the best dancer on staff and the stables are lucky to have her husband. Still, she knows how to entertain a crowd better than anyone."

Deeya knew about Chanti's dancing skills. The dark-skinned beauty had taken it upon herself to do a dance during one of Deeya's more provocative songs in the back rooms. The woman's body was as perfect as a goddess' body, and she had trained it to move in ways that could have sparked wars between nations. While remembering Chanti's dance, from a few years back, Deeya simply raised an eyebrow and commented on Tessa's words, "I always thought your staff were all single...."

Tessa cut Deeya off by saying, "So they'd be more available to my clientele, you mean?"

Deeya heard the mock indignation in Tessa's tone and watched her take a long pull off of her cigar before replying, "And you, yourself."

Tessa laughed at the comment and smoke billowed out of her mouth with the melodic sound of her laughing. Tessa smiled luridly at Deeya, when she had finished with her mirth and said, "Oh, Bard, my staff can do whatever they want, whenever they want, with whoever they want. If they want to be married they can. If they want to be exclusive sexual partners, I don't encroach on their morals. It just so happens that the entire staff enjoys a promiscuous lifestyle."

Deeya then raised her mug of ale that she had sipped on the entire time she had been sitting at the table with Tessa and toasted, "To enjoying one's lifestyle."

Tessa snatched up her goblet of whiskey, stood up, raised the gilded cup to the entire tavern room, and bellowed out, "To enjoying one's lifestyle!"

Everyone in the entire room, except the bards raised their drinks in return and, in unison, yelled, "Here, here!"

Watching everyone empty their drinks and slam their receptacles upon their respective tables had an inspiring effect upon the entire room. Upon slamming down her own goblet, Tessa put on her best bawdy smile and said, "Let us retire, Bard, there are things we need to discuss, and I hope Chanti has already delivered my liquid courage...."

They climbed the spiral staircase single file and walked the catwalk side by side. Tessa waved at the patrons that noticed her, winking at those that seemed to be making a jest to their companions at her bringing the Emerald Bard to her private room. The catwalk ended at a door and beyond that door was a narrow hallway. The left side of the hallway was solid glass which looked out towards the long road heading into the dark forest in the westerly direction. Against the wall opposite the expansive window a set of beautifully ornate doors were set into a dark wall. It was obvious that the doors were carved to represent a scene from history that Deeya was not familiar with. At first glance it was an orgy of flesh, nude men and women pleasuring each other in all sorts of ways. But there were deeper meanings. At the top of the doors sat what looked to be thrones with a king and queen atop them. They held goblets that were being filled from fountains of liquid that looked to be traced down to the people that were engorging on each other's sexual desires. Not sexual fluids, as the Deeya's eyes to be coming from vital areas of the character's bodies. It almost tickled a story Deeya had once heard, but she could not bring the thought forward.

Tessa pushed the doors open and strode boldly into her room. Chanti was there placing a tall bottle of dark liquid on a table with two short glasses. Deeya followed Tessa into the room, trying to take it all in as Tessa thanked and told Chanti that she was free to go, after she closed the curtains to all the windows. Chanti gracefully glided around the room, sliding all the curtains shut. Deeya was distracted from looking around the room by the thought of Tessa sending Chanti away, as she thought that Tessa had been alluding to having Chanti dance for them both up here, if not offer more services.... Deeya did not want them, but she expected them, as she expected a great many of sexual advances from the owner of the inn. Deeya, for the first time, started to truly wonder what this meeting involved, and if she herself might need some "liquid courage" as Tessa had called it.

Chanti closed the doors behind herself, only after striding by Deeya, making the bard fully aware of the dancer's keen sexuality by flashing the bard a lurid smile on her way out. The image of Chanti's swaying body lingered in Deeya's mind as she tried to concentrate on the room around her. The suite was ornate and lush. The windows did have a great view of all the rooms below, when she peeked between the soft, silk curtains. Tessa ignored Deeya, pouring a glass full of the dark liquid and draining the glass quickly. The ceiling appeared to have large skylights, allowing the moons and stars above to spill their pale light upon the plushly carpeted floor below the bard's feet. Treasures from all corners of the world sat on tables illuminated by flickering candles. Deeya was drawn to a statue that she immediately recognized. She picked up the figurine representing a Monk of Drakaara from a monastery called Sanctuary that had played a major part in her life. The bard turned the statue over in her hands, studying the intricacy of the carving's designs in the light from the candles. She recognized the language scribbled on the base of the statue and turned to comment about it to Tessa.

Tessa stopped the bard from commenting by saying something as simple as, "Deeya, I'm sure you've guessed by now…I'm not human."

Deeya stood in stunned silence for a moment that seemed like an eternity to the human looking woman who just confessed her deepest secret. The bard put the figurine down, forgetting its importance, forgetting to even make a mental note to ask about it later, and looked at the human looking woman there in the room with her. The candlelight played off her alabaster skin beautifully while her long, dark, curly hair framed the somber expression that played across her undeniably gorgeous face. The shadows played along the soft expanse of Tessa's purposefully exposed skin, giving her an almost fragile etherealness. For a moment, Tessa seemed a relic from the world where gods had existed, before they had fled to parts unknown.

Her left hand moved up her side seductively, in a fashion that made her look entirely feminine and entirely vulnerable. She stood, like a statue of a goddess, staring past the empty glass in her right hand to the bottle of liquor on the table in front of her. Then her eyes, which better suited a dreamy lover than a tavern owner, rose to meet Deeya's green-eyed gaze.

Deeya replied the only way she could. The bard simply nodded an affirmative.

Movement 3: The Obbligato of Revelation

Tessa took in a deep breath, like it was the first she had taken after a very long time underneath the waves of a body of water. She looked down at Deeya's boots, unable to fully confront what she was saying head on, "I have never discussed this with anyone, and only a handful of people know my secret. But you, my Bard," she continued as she met Deeya's eyes again with a determined expression, "are about to become the only person living I have said these words aloud to."

Deeya blinked for the first time and looked down at the ground, "Tess," she called her for the first time ever, "Why in the world would you chose me to tell?"

Tessa smirked. She sat down her glass and stared into Deeya's green eyes as she firmly said, "Do *not* be coy with me, Bard." Without letting her gaze fall out of Deeya's eyes, Tessa started unstrapping her clothing. "I know damn well that you are far more than what you claim to be." Her belts and straps fell to the ground, as her loose black shirt fell around her waist. Tessa stood, her body nude from the waist up, revealing a sculpture of strength and soft beauty laid bare, every breath she took caused the rise and fall of her chest to seem almost ceremonial.

But Deeya's eyes stayed locked with Tessa's steely blue gaze as the human looking woman continued to reveal not just skin, but a history long hidden beneath clothing and control. "You hold a magic that has been unused in this world since my kind ruled a kingdom," she continued.

Tessa unfastened her leather pants and simply let them fall away from the curves of her hips along with the shirt. "And I need you, you alone. I need you more than I've needed any of my lovers, all save one in particular." She wore nothing underneath her outer clothes. She stepped out of the clothing that piled on the floor at her feet, stark naked, hairless except her eyebrows and glorious mane. Tessa was a breathtaking contradiction, beautifully sculpted too perfectly, like a dream fashioned to tempt mortal hearts. Every curve seemed deliberate, designed to captivate and lure. She seemed a creature shaped not by nature, but by desire itself. Strength and eroticism were woven into every line and curve of her body, and it was impossible to look away from. Yet above all other adjectives that could even come close to describing the beauty before Deeya, Tessa was, at that very moment, vulnerable.

Deeya asked the only question she found herself capable of asking. "What do you need of me?"

"Use your music, use what you use to see hidden magic, use it on me."

Deeya approached the beautiful naked woman, removed her gloves, and held out her bare hands. But she did not touch the pale skin of the woman who admitted to not being human, no matter how that woman craved the bard's soft touch in that moment. No, Deeya held her hands an inch away from skin that was aching for her contact. Seeing such beauty was steadily igniting a fire within the bard she could not deny, but still resisted. Right now she had to go to work. The bard simply hummed. A nice tune, a casual tune, one that you would imagine walking to while you were out and about. Tessa reacted instantly with a shuddering gasp as her feet raised off the floor. She found herself enthralled in magical ecstasy that levitated her inches off the floor just as her hair lifted away from her upper body, revealing the entirety of her skin, pale and alight with quiet, impossible magic, as the bard's musical magic caressed her in ways that no lover ever could. "That's it, Bard, see what I truly am."

Tessa had never been so uniquely exposed in her entire life. A life that spanned more years than even Tessa herself could tally. Tessa did not realize she was opening her legs, a silent plea wrapped in revelation and trust. Deeya could see beyond the gesture, she wasn't baring her body, she was wanting her deepest secret to be revealed. "What are you?"

The words escaped Deeya's lips without the bard even realizing she was thinking it. Tessa's entire body was covered in glowing runes, every curve accentuated, like sacred glyphs etched into a living canvas. Calligraphy drawn by a lover, or a god.

She circled around Tessa's body to look at the back side. Tessa's hair was completely floating, exposing her upper back. Deeya studied her backside, not because Tessa had an amazingly toned rear end, but because the runes that ran up her back told a story. Tessa's voice came in ragged breaths as she said, "You know what I am, you know the stories."

"It can't be."

"It is, Deeya."

"I've only heard the stories," Deeya whispered as she studied the lines of magic across Tessa's luscious body. "I heard they were all wiped out."

A tear escaped Tessa's right eye. Deeya had walked all the way around Tessa's floating body, until she was standing in front of the woman again. Deeya's bare hand, still a scant inch from Tessa's glowing skin, followed a line from her groin, across her toned stomach, until her hand hovered just below Tessa's chest, which rose and fell like something afloat in a still sea. Deeya's music touched Tessa more thoroughly than Deeya's hand ever could, and as Tessa imagined she could feel Deeya's hand firmly grasp her firm breast, Deeya caught sight of the tear creeping down Tessa's cheek. The bard studied how the tear followed a magical line that seemed to glow brighter as it followed the curve of Tessa's jaw and down her throat, a path illuminated by magic and sorrow both, as if grief itself had carved magic into her flesh.

"Every last one of us," she replied to Deeya's statement.

Deeya continued her walk around Tessa's body, it was a canvas of art, but all that art pointed to one thing, and one thing only. If she had cast this spell on a Fae, she would have seen similar designs, as they were beings created from magic. Each line not only followed muscles and sinew below the skin, but the magical lines that actually stitched their being together. Fae lived off of a magic that created life, it built up inside of them, and they had to release it into living things around them or else they would die. That is why they were the keepers of forests; they gave forests life. But this...this was something else. Deeya stopped at Tessa's side and closed the inch that separated their skin and touched a line by Tessa's ear with a single finger. "This line, this line means."

Tessa gasped at the touch and started saying yes in an almost moaning way. "Yes, Deeya.... Yes...."

Deeya traced the line down Tessa's throat, the line got brighter as Deeya's finger caressed it, almost as if she was helping paint on the canvas of skin. "This line...," she whispered as the line went down Tessa's neck, across her collarbone, around the outside of her breast, around her back, and around the muscles of her firm rear. Tessa was almost panting, her body looked as though it was drawn taut like a bow, as her hair and breasts floated as if she were suspended in water. "This line means you are...."

To Deeya's eyes, the lines on Tessa's skin all pointed to something she dare not say aloud. It was the inverse of how the magic that held the Fae together worked. This magic would absorb life, taking it within, sustaining the soul that was almost trapped underneath the alluring flesh that encompassed the undeniable beauty that was Tessa's nude body.

Tessa's breath was ragged, and when finally admitted it out loud, her voice actually broke. It was something she had not said in so long that she almost choked saying it, but finally she let the words escape her full, licentious lips, "I am a vampire."

All the magical lines turned from yellow to blue in a flaring, almost blinding display, as Tessa's orgasm reached a climax that outshone the seemingly dim light of the candles, the moons, and the stars. Deeya quickly pulled away her finger, as if she was bitten. In her shock at the words, she also stopped humming and Tessa abruptly fell unceremoniously to the floor. She had only been a handful of inches above the plush carpet, but Deeya's magic, which had been intimately caressing every inch of Tessa's trembling form, had been the only thing holding her up at all. She crumpled upon the floor like a doll and looked up at the Bard with destroyed blue eyes that were shedding tears. "As far as I know, I'm the last vampire, and I'm no longer even a vampire…."

Deeya wanted to take a step back. Vampires had been wiped out centuries ago. They had lived in a kingdom far to the south, ruling as they willed. Brutal, blood hungry, they survived off of the blood of any living creature.

Deeya *really* wanted to take a step back. She remembered the carving adorning the entrance to this very room, portraying an orgy of sexuality and blood. That made her remember why vampires had been removed from the world in a huge bloody battle. Once upon a time all the kingdoms united under a single cause, one of the three times such a thing had ever occurred in historical records. The cause being a common enemy that needed to be warred against with the might of an entire world. The most dangerous enemy ever known.

Now, all that danger, all that strength, crumpled into a trembling shape at Deeya's feet, weeping for a salvation that Deeya could not give. Every instinct told Deeya to run, to fight, to stay alive, anything....
Anything but kneel down, wrap her arms around the broken, indecent, impossibly dangerous, prurient creature and hold the thing the world had once rightly feared. A creature that cried like a child into the bard's comforting bosom. But that's exactly what Deeya found herself doing....

It was rare to find the Emerald Bard without words. Yet Deeya struggled to find the right thing to say. She knew the story went deeper, would go deeper, she just had to allow this living paradox of strength, sorrow, sexuality, and vulnerability trembling against her, to get there. Deeya put her cheek on the top of Tessa's head and rocked her a bit, saying, "It's okay, Tess, I'm here to help."

But Tessa kept sobbing. Deeya wondered why she was suddenly calling the woman Tess and regretted even more not being able to hone those motherly instincts she should have gotten a chance to upon becoming a mother, but that was another story, and not important right now. Deeya stroked Tessa's thick, curly, black hair as she tried not to overanalyze the situation. Which would be far too easy to do. It could still all be an elaborate trap to kill Deeya and drink her blood, right?

That idea, though, got her thinking, trying to remember the stories she had heard about vampires.

The only ones that came vividly to her mind were the tales she was told in her childhood. Deeya had grown up a homeless street urchin in a city that had been ravaged by the falling of the sky, there had been constant worry of plague, which led to worry about the return of the vampires. It was a common theme during that time, to scare people into staying in at night, a makeshift curfew that helped to keep the crime rate down. Or at least that's how she saw it as a child who needed to steal bread to eat.

Finally, Tessa sniffed and said, "You must think I'm so weak...."

Tessa started to pull away, trying to cover her nakedness. Deeya shook her head, "On the contrary, you said it yourself.... I cannot imagine how devastating it is for you to say what you said out loud."

Tessa gave her a sincere look from under her curly locks that were now in disarray. "Not many people have gotten the pleasure of holding me while I cry."

Deeya smiled and stood. She walked to the bed and pulled the cover off of it. Tessa stood under her own power as Deeya wrapped her in the thick furry lining. Tessa pulled it close to her exposed skin, enveloping herself within the plush and comforting warmth, like she was seeking shelter against a winter's day. Deeya petted Tessa's black hair and said, "Are you ready to tell me the whole story?"

Tessa walked over to the bottle on the table, trailing the blanket behind her on the ground. "I hope so...I don't know if I can break like that again."

Deeya saw her weak smile and warned, "Only one more drink, you've already had so much you've stripped for me."

Tessa laughed, still holding the cover tight in front of her, even though it was hanging off one of her shoulders. "Oh, Bard, if you knew how much I craved you.... I am accustomed to bedding whomever I want, on the spot. And the second time we met, you played a love song that touched me...." Tears started welling up in her eyes again. Deeya stepped forward and started pouring her another glass of the dark liquid. Tessa watched the bard perform the smallest of tasks to assist her and mused out loud, "It all starts and ends with love, does it not?"

Deeya wiped the tears from Tessa's cheeks as she held out the glass with her other hand. Tessa reached out from under the cover, and a flash of bare skin slipped free. Sure, Deeya had already seen more than enough to know what she was missing, and yet, even the hint of exposed skin drew her eye before she could stop herself. Deeya tried to ignore the slip and replied to Tessa's musing, "I ofttimes believe so."

Tessa downed the drink. "You know...he was the only one who ever called me 'Tess.' In fact, that's where I got the name I use now."

Deeya took the empty glass from Tessa and sat it upon the table. Tessa turned and walked towards the bed, stopping short of it to sit in the fancy cushioned bench that stood at the foot of the bed. She sat gingerly on it, trying to keep the cover around her. She continued in an almost masculine, matter of fact voice, "My one true love." She paused to sniff at the comment as if it were some form of inside joke. "He was my childhood servant, Silus. Seems so silly now, our trying to hide our relationship...."

Tessa stopped to look at Deeya, who was still standing. Deeya took the hint and turned a chair at the table to face Tessa, positioning herself close enough to be touched. Deeya then said, "You can never choose who you fall in love with."

"Oh trust me, I've heard that line." Tessa then smirked, as if she was about to win an unspoken game. "You've been in love with two women in the recent past, last I heard."

Deeya turned a dark shade of red. Her love life, or lack thereof was never something she enjoyed discussing, but then...this was a uniquely intimate situation. Tessa leaned back, having finally gotten an upper hand. It was always about a game with her, but then, that was just who she was. As she leaned back, she lifted her very bare legs and stretched them across the bench, a deliberate display that Deeya tried, and failed, not to notice. Deeya knew from Tessa's posture, which spoke of comfort and confidence, like a queen in command of a private audience, that she was inviting Deeya to move her head slightly to the side, so she could have a commanding view of the heaven she was promising. Tessa even let the cover slip down her shoulder more, fully allowing her exhibitionism to seep back into the situation.

"You could say that, I guess...."

Tessa laughed, "From what I hear you are, or at least were, in love with a tall blond elf who vanished one day after you disappointed her, and a dark-skinned half-elven wild girl who dresses like a wolf. She turned out to be a wild child who loved the call of the wild more than the thought of a tame existence as your pet."

Deeya sighed, thinking about the two women who ruled her heart. The one, Ashengrey, a sorceress of sorts who could manipulate time. Deeya and Ash had not parted well, but it had been decades since they had last communicated. And that communication had been a letter which firmly ended any words the two had to say to each other. The other, Aloucia, was a wild girl indeed, with chocolate skin and snow white hair. They made an interesting dichotomy, being the lady and the wolf, respectively. "How do they compare with the one you speak of?"

Tessa's smile remained, but it changed, as if she turned somber, as she remembered something distant. "He was something special, from a rare lineage, a shapeshifter, some called them. Many vampires don't have special powers as the stories now suggest. But some of us...some of us did. In his true form, he was a majestic, perfectly built man with a cock that filled me perfectly...." Deeya noticed a lewd movement below the cover, as if Tessa was caressing her breasts at the memory. "But he could take any form he wanted...any form I wanted." Tessa then locked eyes with Deeya, "He is the reason I am able to love a woman as well as I do."

Deeya nodded, "That would be an amazing gift, especially in a lover. What happened to him?"

Tessa sighed, visibly moving her unseen hand away from her still covered breasts as she said, "That's not where this story begins...."

Deeya then said, "Well, let's start at the beginning and get to where we need to get to. You still haven't told me what you need of me, besides your cravings."

Tessa laughed, sounding like herself again. Powerful and in control. Tessa shifted, just enough to let the blanket fall, revealing a sumptuous glimpse of pale skin. A calculated move, daring Deeya to look anywhere but the 'accidental' flash. "I know you are tempted, Bard," she said, covering herself again. "Yes, I want to possess you, even if just for one night. I want to hear you call out my name in that melodic voice of yours, as I force you into an orgasm that you remember all your days." As she talked, she quite obviously slid her hand down the length of her body. Tessa parted the plush, fur lined cover with deliberate ease, revealing the curve of her breasts, the taut line of her stomach, and the undeniable hunger written into every inch of her body. Her fingers moved between her thighs, bold and unashamed, as her gaze pinned Deeya in place. The rhythm of her touch sending a visible shudder through her frame. She punctuated her sensual masturbation with the words, "Then have you use that tongue to...."

"Tessa, let's not get distracted, you obviously needed my skills for something more urgent than a simple fuck."

Tessa frowned, pulled her hand away from her groin area, covered the body she had been exposing, and held her fingers up to her nose. She inhaled the aroma coming from her glistening fingers as she watched Deeya like a hawk. "It's a shame to waste it when it is wet, you know."

Deeya raised an eyebrow and said, "Who were you, in the beginning."

"I was a Countess, Countess...Countess...." Tessa looked shocked for a minute, forgetting her fingers, the aroma of her own sex, and her own lewd behavior as she turned her thoughts introspectively inward, looking for the name. "I've...I've forgotten...."

Deeya said, "How long has it been?"

Tessa looked at Deeya and said, "At least a thousand years...." She looked around at her room with an almost numb expression. "It might be getting close to two thousand years," she said in a voice that exposed her thoughts as being drawn to the furthest reaches that memory can go.

"So you were a Countess?"

Tessa nodded, getting back on track. "*The* Countess. My eldest sister's husband was the king. I had a place of high honor as I grew up. I was treated like a princess, even had my own servant. He was an orphan and was handpicked because of his abilities to be my servant and companion, as he would be the best at protecting me as we grew up. I lived in that palace, as my family ruled for all the short years of my childhood. I remember not even being considered an adult as the war that ended us broke out."

"What happened to start the war?"

Tessa sighed, "The true story was that one of the clans got in trouble with the elves, your woodland elves, if I remember right. It is so hard to tell since the tribes of elves have split, moved, reformed, and split again during all the time since. I know your ancestors finally settled upon that island, with the forest that predates history. It was once too sacred a place for any living being to set foot on…."

Deeya nodded, "But they had no other place to go. Human expansion felled the rest of the habitable sacred forests."

Tessa said, "Yes, but long before that, a chief of one of the elven tribes fell in love with a vampire female. They accused her of seducing him. As I said, it always begins and ends with love." Deeya nodded somberly to the lightly repeated words. She had known many tales whose fates were decided by someone falling in love with the wrong person at the wrong time. Tessa continued, "The elven tribe went into a frenzy, which caused a skirmish. When blood was drank after battle outside of their tribe's borders, a treaty was said to have been broken. Fearing that we were going to overrun the world the kingdoms united."

"Just like that?"

Tessa laughed, "No, it is never that simple. But after a few decades, after many skirmishes, many demands, my brother-in-law, as the humans would have me call him, unleashed what the world feared. Many people in many places were killed to send a message. The message though, turned out to be the death warrant, as it signed the treaty that brought everyone together against us."

Deeya sat in silence, watching Tessa talk. This was history, this was sadness, this was the destruction of a world that was. She continued, "The war got to our castle, our last stronghold. I watched as the trebuchets and catapults hurled magical bombs further than the magic users could cast their own destruction. Finally, the decision was made and we rode out."

Tessa looked at Deeya, looking her directly in the eyes, "You should have seen me, Deeya, having just become an adult. I was resplendent in my vampric armor. You would have sung a song about me that day. About all of us. Instead of dying in our homes, we rode out, on the wings of giant bats."

Deeya smiled slight, "That paints an amazing picture in the mind's eye."

Tessa's smile turned sad as she said, "It was an amazing site, until we were decimated. Vampires are not magic users. Sure, we had the occasional 'power.' Swift speed, amazing strength, ability to change form, but magic...we had none of that. Many of us burned." Tessa then turned straight up somber, somber with such a sadness that it seemed as if the candles in the room got darker. "Silus burned...."

Deeya tensed at the words, not knowing if she should say anything at all. Yet, "I'm sorry," escaped her own lips.

Tessa's shrugged and said, "That's what I get for riding him into battle instead of our typical bat steeds. But that's also how I didn't die." Tessa looked into Deeya's eyes, "While we were falling together, and he being on fire, he clutched me to his chest and took all the impact." Tessa continued her stare, allowing Deeya to look deep into her soul, "When I awoke, his burnt natural body lay next to me, holding me. My body was broken in so many ways, yet nowhere near as broken as Silus's. Realization washed over me, as I laid there, dying, looking at the destroyed corpse of the being I loved with all my heart. And then…the strangest thing happened."

Deeya waited for the space of time to close, but Tessa had stopped, frozen still. She urged the story onwards, breaking Tessa's reverie, "What happened, Tess?"

A single tear escaped Tessa's left eye as her gaze focused on something somewhere far behind Deeya. "An angel came down from the heavens. He was tall and handsome with flowing black hair and jet black wings. A ray of light from the sun parted the clouds behind the stark figure of this god descending upon the earth and landed upon him from behind, casting a halo to shimmer around his winged form. He landed gracefully beside me, knelt down beside my broken body, which I could no longer even feel. I felt nothing but the creeping cold of death as it slowly settled over me." Tessa snuggled into her blanket again, seeking the warmth to escape the frigid memory of every living beings worst fear. Another tear escaped as she refocused her wet eyes on Deeya, "Just his being next to me, warmed me somehow. He judged me in that moment, I could tell by his eyes. With my life slipping away from me, he asked the one question I feared he would ask. He asked me if I wanted to live."

Tears flowed freely from Tessa's eyes as she continued, "How could I possibly say yes, Deeya? My one true love was dead beside me, a ruin of a corpse."

Deeya shook her head saying, "You couldn't."

Then the angel spoke again, and asked me if I wanted to live with my lover by my side. I ask you, Deeya, how could I possibly say no?"

Deeya still shook her head and repeated, "You couldn't."

Tessa sighed, wiped her eyes, looked away from Deeya, and said, "He made me a deal, it sounded fair enough. I would stay next to the angel for the rest of eternity, sharing his power with mine, and my power with his. Silus would be there as well, always by my side...." She found that suddenly, she had to breathe in, and that breath shook her entire soul.

Deeya took the opportunity to ask, "What happened?"

Tessa's eyes met Deeya's again. Within those eyes, Deeya could see Tessa's spirit, stoic, hard...determined. She then got up, taking the cover with her, to her pile of clothes she had discarded from her body earlier. She bent over and picked up her shirt, intentionally angling herself so that Deeya would have a view that most men, and some women, yearned for their entire lives. Deeya fought the instinct to glance away, not wanting to give ground in the flirtatious war Tessa was waging. Deeya saw the erotic display for what it was, another layer of Tessa's armor she wielded without effort. And hated how much she enjoyed looking.

Tessa stood back up and unceremoniously slipped the shirt back on while saying, "I hope you don't mind me putting this back on, I have to show you something."

The loose shirt draped across Tessa's form, doing little to conceal her. The size of the shirt was not what Deeya expected, it came down far enough to cover her hips, also had a plunging neckline that exposed Tessa's belly held together with what looked like boot straps.

Normally the shirt was bunched and twisted about her torso and hung off her shoulders.

Tessa caught Deeya looking at her midriff. Deeya simply said, "No, I don't mind."

Tessa grinned a grin that showed Tessa's want to be playful, but the face that framed the grin showed a look of appreciation for being appreciated. "Good, it's a slight bit chilly where I'm taking you."

Movement 4: Into the Darkness

Deeya watched as Tessa ambled over to one of the wardrobes, opened it, pushed the clothing aside, and stepped through, vanishing from sight. Deeya followed quickly once she realized that it had to be a secret door.

The hallway on the other side was dark beyond belief. Tessa said, "Care to create light?"

Deeya obliged. It was a straightforward magical song. Three bars of music, hummed or sung, though sung made the light last longer, and poof, there was a floating orb of light. After the three bars of music ended, the light started to slowly fade away. After several seconds Deeya had to sing or hum the verse again. This concept was how most of the magical music Deeya knew worked. She could actually sing multiple songs, stringing them together causing multiple effects. Or she could simply sing one every now and then, and talk.

Tessa smiled at the light, "Amazing, Bard, simply amazing. A lost art has been rediscovered...." She then groped Deeya's backside without shame. "And you wonder why I crave you."

Deeya smirked and slapped Tessa's hand away. She decided to ignore the game for now, as a more serious business was at hand. "How much do you know about this lost art, as you call it?"

Tessa grinned, a very knowing and flirtatious grin, "Let's not get ahead of ourselves." She sauntered past the globe into the darkness beyond, "Follow me, Bard."

Deeya hummed a bit to set the glowing orb in motion pushing it out a few feet ahead and above Tessa, as the bard followed behind her. Deeya kept her gaze fixed forward, trying not to let Tessa's careless grace distract her from the darkness at the edge of her light. The movement of Tessa's hips and the brush of her shirt tugged at Deeya's senses regardless. Every now and then she hummed the same tones to keep the globe of light in existence.

When both women were in stride together, almost side by side, Tessa told Deeya to make the globe move a ways ahead of them. The globe itself stayed in relative position to Deeya, so as they started to descend stairs, it moved downwards with her. After a couple of steps down the stairs, and both women got their footing on the slightly wet stone, Tessa continued the story, "The angel, as he still appeared to me, flew me and the carcass of my lover here, to this cave. It was a long forgotten forest, most traveled leagues out of the way to avoid it. In fact, there were port cities to the North and South that exist to this day because this forest was the end of the line for trade caravans."

Deeya asked, "What was so bad about the forest?"

Deeya could hear Tessa's smile in her voice as she said, "It was reportedly haunted, but honestly it was a den for giant forest spiders, along with all the wretchedness that comes along with that sort of foulness."

Deeya then said, "Liches and other forms of undead?"

Tessa nodded, "Yeah, nasty things. This cave was his home, right in the middle of the forest. There are all sorts of amenities here, the natural hot springs, the underground water system that allows for refrigeration of food, the river nearby...."

"All things you utilize within the Deal to great effect, making the inn itself a place with many amenities one normally doesn't find upon the road."

"Exactly, but then, there wasn't an inn. The inn, it turned out, was part of the deal itself. I'm an eternal being, as long as I get sustenance. I'll never age. He knew, that through that power, he could live off of my essence for the rest of eternity. Not only that, but combining my vampric powers with his power of being able to absorb life forces, as he was going to absorb mine, we were going to have the perfect place to live off of the land, as it were."

Deeya blinked, "So the inn is part of the terms? What were all the terms with the deal?"

Tessa smirked, "At that time, he was apparently still coming up with all the terms." She then cocked her head to the side, thinking about it more and said, "Or he knew what he wanted and he was just twisting the right words at the right time to bait me."

Deeya sighed and shook her head. They were finally coming to the end of the stairs that seemed to go on for some time. Then Tessa slipped. The last step was a bit of a drop, and the wetness of it made it slicker than the rest of the steps had been. The soles of Deeya's boots held firm, but Tessa's bare feet did not. Deeya jumped out and caught Tessa, righting her quickly. It wasn't until they locked eyes that Deeya became aware of where her hand was, and what it was grasping. Tessa then seized Deeya's hand and kept it on her firm right breast. Deeya sighed and did not resist what Tessa was doing. She just looked her right in the eyes. "Really?" she asked in a flat tone

Tessa smiled and let go of Deeya's hand. "Anyone that saves my life like that deserves a free grope."

Deeya took her hand back, knowing that the touch had been had and would in no way be forgotten. She gestured forward with the same hand, trying to set aside the lingering sensation. "I believe you were telling a story...," she said, trying to change the subject.

Tessa left the shirt hanging off one of her shoulders. Even though it still covered her, Tessa was still trying to tempt attention, causing Deeya to force herself to look elsewhere. "Where was I, before you saved my life and got me all hot and bothered with your soft hand?"

A mirthful smirk spread across Deeya's face as she shook her head in the negative to point out the vampress's audaciousness. "The terms, I believe."

"Ah," Tessa said. She started walking again and Deeya fell into step beside her, keeping her eyes forward, forcing herself to ignore the way Tessa moved. Or how the too-loose shirt did little to hide her form. "His final terms were something like this: He would put Silus into a specific pool of water within the cave that would heal him and keep him alive and one day he'd step out fully healed. He would get his minions to build the inn, which I would run. The people that would frequent the inn, after the forest was more or less cleaned of its evil, would give me a way to sustain myself off the life force of others without having to skulk and destroy lives. I would share this power with him through a sexual ritual, every time the Wolf's Moon bloomed full in the sky. All three of us would live in this location together, in this perfectly peaceful arrangement."

The Wolf's Moon was one of three moons that appeared in the night's sky. It was a very regular moon, going through a twenty-eight day cycle, never wavering. It was also the moon that the wolves chose to howl at every month, as it was always the biggest and brightest of the three. Tessa added, "In the time of my people, we called it the Woman's Blood Moon, did you know?"

Deeya shook her head, "No, I didn't, but it makes sense," with the human female's cycle of blood.

Tessa sighed, "The angel was a handsome man, Deeya. I looked upon his features and physique and knew I would have no problems giving myself to this man. In my fanciful imaginations, I pictured myself ravaging him, wrapped in those gloriously beautiful wings, far more than once a month."

"When did it all go wrong?"

Tessa stopped and looked down at the ground in front of her, "The instant I signed."

Deeya stopped as well, turning her body to face Tessa. Tessa was a head taller than Deeya and quite striking in her vulnerability. Deeya felt a need to comfort her, to help her in some way, but she could not fathom how, as Tessa seemed to be reliving a horror deep inside herself.

"He changed, right in front of my eyes, into his true form."

Deeya frowned, "His true form?"

Tessa seemed to not even hear what Deeya had asked. Instead, the memory she was reliving was causing her to fall further into a disassociation with her surroundings. She continued on, though, as the memory was forcing her to relay the information she seemed too horrified by to speak out loud, "He changed while I was fucking him."

Deeya gasped, instantly realizing that the pact they signed was sealed with some kind of binding sexual magic. It was a type of magic that bred the concept of the consummation of a marriage.

Without warning, Tessa came back from the memory and looked into Deeya's eyes again. The light from the orb, a few feet away, cast shadows and reflections into Tessa's piercing blue eyes. She looked as haunted as the forest surrounding the inn had reportedly once been. When she finally spoke, the words came from an empty part of her soul, echoing hollowly off the walls of the cavern surrounding them, which were outside of the light's radius. "He's a spider."

Deeya blinked, not understanding what she just heard. "A…. Wait…. No…."

Tessa did not blink as Deeya's face drained of blood, becoming as white as a sheet under the pale orb's fading light. Tessa's voice echoed again, off the unseen walls, more forceful, "He's a spider demon. Eight legs, eight eyes, just...just...," her matter-of-fact tone finally faded away into not being able to speak about the horror.

Deeya absolutely did not know what to say to this revelation. She had no clue how to act. She just stood there, shocked. Tessa finally shook herself back, wiped away her own tears, breathed in a shuddering breath for her own strength before saying, "But, compared to everything else, that isn't the worst of it."

"How the fuck can *that* not be the worst of it," Deeya asked under her breath? Tessa took a few steps backwards, away from Deeya, as the sound of Deeya's near whispered curse echoed oddly around the two women. Deeya then took two steps to catch up to Tessa and saw it....

It looked like a waterfall of frozen glass and behind the glass was an amazingly beautiful man. Looking like a perfect statue, vulnerable in his stillness, muscles carved in impossible precision, with every line of his body laid bare. His silver hair billowed outward from his head and was so long that it vanished into the haze of the glass like water. Tessa looked up at him, resting her hand on the solid, rippled surface between her former lover and herself. As Deeya stepped closer, she made the orb refresh its brightness and rise up above the pair of women, letting the light shine into the hazy cylinder, so that both could see inside more clearly. "He's alive in there, Deeya. Alive, but in some form of suspension."

Deeya, again, could not speak. How could she have anything to say at a moment such as this? It was tragic, heart breaking, and soul crushing. She put her hand on Tessa's bare shoulder. The vampric woman's skin was cold to the touch. "Tess...," she said softly.

"He is the only other person to ever call me that."

"I don't even know why I started calling you that. I guess I felt close enough to shorten your name like I shorten mine to Deeya for friends."

Tessa smiled, but did not look back to Deeya. "He shortened my title from Countess to Tessa, and then when we were alone, to Tess."

Deeya sighed loudly, remembering the story that Tessa was in the middle of. "So the demon tricked you with words? Silus is still alive and forever beside you, but forever out of reach...."

Tessa nodded absently. She finally turned to Deeya, her shirt had fallen off one shoulder, completely exposing a breast. Oddly, it was not erotic in the slightest, it just made her seem that much more vulnerable. "I found a way to kill the demon, Deeya, but I need your help."

Deeya pulled her hand back from Tessa's bare shoulder and said, "What do you need me to do?"

Tessa smiled, "I can do nothing but commend you on your beautiful loyalty to your friends, dear Bard." She shook her head, still holding the smile and said, "But seriously, you should never jump into the water without knowing how deep it is."

Deeya smirked in a rueful way, "It's what I do, Tess."

Tessa smiled warmly and reached a hand up to stroke Deeya's cheek, a warm gesture, the movement of which made the shirt re-cover her exposed breast. "I'm going to ask you to risk your life, along with mine, and...," she turned her head slightly, gesturing to Silus, "most likely his."

Deeya sighed and ran a hand through her short hair. "And it's worth the risk?"

"Deeya," Tessa said slightly, taking her hand back, crossing her arms under her breasts, causing them to press together, "every month I have to fuck a huge demon spider. Not only is it huge, Deeya, but he has become morbidly obese off of how much he feeds. I have to fuck this disgusting mound of flesh with eight legs and eight eyes.

"He saves himself until I cum and he can tell if I'm faking. As I do, he absorbs the vampric magic from my body. He uses this magic to absorb the life force of people with a certain area from this spot, it could be miles for all I know. He only takes a little bit from all those people, so no one notices. Deeya, he is absorbing your life force, right now.

"When he has milked my orgasm for as long as he wants, which can sometimes be for tens of minutes, he fills me with his seed. His seed is acid, Deeya, as it leaks out, it makes the skin on my inner thighs sizzle and blister. I cannot, nor will I, describe the internal pain."

Deeya stood in stoic silence, her facial expression exuding shock during the entire commentary. She had never experienced so much revelation that left her speechless. Tessa continued, "Thankfully, the parts of my vampric powers that he doesn't take allow me to heal fast. I can be back in bed with someone worth fucking in a few days."

Deeya shook her head, "How does the absorbing work?"

Tessa shrugged and said, "Mainly it has to do with how vampires actually feed. I'm sure you've heard stories, how we drink blood and get sustenance from that, but that's not the whole truth. Your essence, your soul is attached to your blood. As it leaks from you, vampires ingest the living blood, which is still directly linked to your life force, and absorb your soul's power. It feeds the magic within us, as we are completely magical beings, like the Fae."

Deeya nodded, the Fae have to add their life force to nature, or they die. Helping a tree grow, helping grass grow, something along those lines, even healing in some cases. It is a power that just builds up inside of them from living. The Fae, and other magical beings, all have origin stories where someone, or something, created them into existence with magic of some sort. Someone very powerful, a very long time ago....

Tessa continued on, "I can no longer feed at all. If I drink blood, it is just great tasting liquid, but nothing more. He has taken my vampric power, used it in this new way by combining it with whatever powers he has, and if I do not go into his lair and offer myself to him during this ritual, then I shan't get what I need to survive. Over the course of the next lunar cycle, I will just wither away and die."

Deeya closed her eyes, took a deep breath, and said, "What do we need to do?"

Tessa unfolded her arms, the loose shirt settling back against her frame, and grabbed Deeya arms, "First, we have to train you, then we have to go over the plan, then we have to succeed in the impossible."

Deeya smirked, "Well, you have a Bard on your side, we kind of specialize in the impossible."

Tessa laughed, "And that's why I chose you."

"What did you mean by training?"

Tessa grinned and teasingly cupped her breast through her shirt, suggestive as ever. "You remember how I said that I know about the Bardic magic of old that was forgotten?"

"Yeah, I've only discovered what I could do by meditation and playing around."

Tessa grinned even wider, groping her own breast in a very self-gratifying way, "Oh, have I got something for you!"

She grabbed Deeya by the hand, using her free hand, and both of them walked briskly back the way they came. When they got back into Tessa's suite, she went to the bench she had laid in before, knelt before it, and pulled a chest out from under it. She unlocked it and opened it slowly. Deeya, who had been standing behind Tessa as she bent over, moved to get a better look at the contents of the chest, as the view she had from behind Tessa was... not what she needed to see right that moment. Inside the chest was a collection of what looked like ancient artifacts. Deeya could see strange armor pieces, daggers, books, vials full of fluid, and coins. Tessa rummaged for a few moments, snared something underneath it all, and said, "There."

She retrieved a small, dusty old book from the chest and handed it to Deeya. Deeya took it and turned it over in her hands while walking to the table to sit. The cover held no distinct markings that she could tell. She laid it upon the table and gingerly opened the fragile cover. What she saw on the title page made her gasp. Tessa smiled broadly, "So, you like it?"

Deeya looked down at the symbol that stood out in gold leaf on the page. It was a treble and bass cleft symbol combined together. The way they were combined almost seemed to make a heart symbol. With awe on her face, the bard looked at Tessa, who was grinning like a giddy little girl. "Do you know what this symbol is?"

Tessa shook her head, "Only that it is the blade of your axe and the magical bards of old used that symbol on their tabards."

Deeya took the axe out of its straps and held it up in front of her face. "This is the Sonnetic Axe. It holds a portion of the destructive power from the plane of music." She then looked at Tessa, "It was given to me by the Goddess of Music...."

Tessa stopped grinning and looked up at Deeya, from here still kneeling position, with reverence, "You are a Chosen?"

Deeya shrugged, "I don't know what anyone calls it. All I know is, I stood in front of the goddess herself, surround by angels."

Tessa bit her lower lip and said, "A real angel...."

As Deeya looked down upon the beautiful woman kneeling beside her, she had a realization. Tessa no longer believed in Angels or Goddesses. All the celestial beings had lost their meaning to her, as she lay in her dungeon, tricked by a demon. Deeya smiled and petted Tessa's hair, "Yes, Tess, there is still good and beauty in the world. We will kill the demon and free you." As she finished her line, she had to stop her face from reacting. She just made a promise to a vampire that she would help release vampires upon the world again…. Tessa trusted her, but could she honestly trust Tessa?

Tessa did not notice the confliction in Deeya's heart and simply snuggled her face into Deeya's hand. Tessa was so happy within herself, knowing that there were actually angels, and this beautiful bard had stood before them herself…that she had to stop herself short from trying to seduce the Emerald Bard again. She pushed the thought of pleasing a Goddess' Chosen out of her mind and said, "Time is short, you should get to reading. The ceremony is tonight."

"As in tonight, tonight," Deeya asked with shock in her voice?

Tessa laughed, "Deeya, the sun is about to rise, it is officially morning."

Deeya sighed in a relieved way, "So, to work then."

Deeya sat at the table and read. She read like her life depended on it. And she learned. Tessa removed the shirt, took a bath, and tried her damnedest to distract Deeya by posing her voluptuous nude body in various positions. Tessa knew that time was of the essence, but she did not want to think about what time was leading to, and she knew a good romp would take her mind off of things.

The book was a detailed account of a particular bard's lifestyle. Deeya thought she might have recognized the name of the bard, but without her old notes she could not be sure. It had biographical information, but mostly it was about the bardic lifestyle of the time. Traveling troubadours that used magic to help people. The magic was special and the songs were listed in detail. It talked about the origins of magical music and of the Goddess of Music herself. It talked about other types of famous bards who passed through history.

Deeya simply skimmed as much as she could, the historical information, she knew, she would have to go over in detail later. Right now, she was looking for any clues that would help her defeat a fully powered demon. Every few pages a song showed up. Each one was a magical song. Among those she found was a healing song better than the one she already learned herself, a song to make her and whomever could hear her run faster, and there was even a song that would remove water from clothing. She was shocked to see some of the songs she had thought she had just made up, the light orb for instance, or the mind control one, or the one that made her invisible. Finally, though, she came across a song that she knew would help.

"Here."

Tessa was still stark naked, she had ordered food from a male staff member who she had fondled under his clothes and kissed deeply. He had just left breathlessly when Deeya called out. Tessa moved to the table with an easy, dangerous grace allowing her nude body to provocatively move in a way that dragged Deeya's thoughts places they had no business going. She finished the movement by leaning over the table, allowing her breasts to dangle below her body creating a display of flesh that Deeya could in no way ignore. "What is it," the lascivious vampire asked?

"This here will make arrows violently explode. I can shoot him from across the room, which I can enter invisibly."

Tessa thought for a minute, then straightened her back, causing her body to move in a way that shocked Deeya, who had been getting used to Tessa's nude body in her relaxed pose. Deeya averted her eyes downward, only to land upon Tessa's crotch. She then looked away completely, trying not to blush, as it seemed no matter where she looked, Tessa was on display somehow. Tessa said, "Yes, okay. I can start the ritual, once he penetrates me, after he lifts me up into position, you can shoot him with your arrow. How big of an explosion?"

Deeya lifted her gaze to meet Tessa's, trying to forget the way Tessa's body had just moved in front of her, though she couldn't hide the warmth in her cheeks. "The book said it would tear a horse in half, split a half size bolder, or fell the largest tree that has ever lived," she said, thinking. "Though I don't think it means the giant trees in Fo'Est."

Tessa nodded to herself, formulating the plan in her head, having not noticed Deeya's accidental arousal. "That will do it. Shoot him in the throat, if you can make it out from his obese spider body." Tessa visibly shivered. "Try to expose his heart but not destroy it. If I finish him myself then I should be able to take my powers from him." She smiled at her plan. "This might actually work."

Deeya shrugged, regaining control her of urges. "I'm sure a thousand things will go wrong."

Tessa turned around and started pacing the room, her bare body moving with a familiar ease that was near maddening. Deeya forced herself to watch, getting a clear view of Tessa moving from all angles, in hopes that if she could get used to the sight again, it wouldn't affect her so. "His minions will attack," Tessa said, never stopping.

"Minions," Deeya asked?

Tessa turned back around and paced more. Watching her body move was a hypnotic experience. "He's a spider demon. He controlled all the spiders in the forest. They are the minions that build this Inn. The haunted forest full of spiders is no longer full of spiders because he called them all down into the cave system below."

Deeya sighed; she hated spiders. "So, we kill him, but his giant spiders will come up and overrun us?"

Tessa tapped her lower lip. "When he dies, his spiders should as well. He's what nourishes them."

Deeya thought it, but did not say it, "Just like you." She bit her cheek to keep from saying it, because it was true. Tessa was just another minion of his.

Tessa then put her hands on the table, facing Deeya. Her breasts swung under her, as she leaned into Deeya's space, voice low and eyes intense. "This might be the last day we have, Deeya."

Deeya sighed and said, "No, Tessa."

Tessa frowned and looked sad, "Please? Please make love to me...."

Deeya stood up, leaving the book on the table, the song, as well as a few others, had already burned into her head. "Tessa, I respect you. I love you like I do all my friends. You truly are beautiful, extremely erotic, and parts of me lust for you. But I no longer give body away for anything less than my soul sharing a beautiful moment with someone else's."

Tessa's eyes started welling up with tears. "This could be my last request...."

Deeya walked around the table and put her arms around the beautiful naked woman. "We should sleep."

"At least hold me," Tessa whispered into Deeya's moderate chest.

"Okay." Deeya stepped back and took off her corset, belt, and straps. Tessa watched with bated breath as Deeya removed her leather pants. Unfortunately, Deeya wore soft underwear under her pants, but it still showed off more of Deeya's body than Tessa had ever seen.

As Deeya walked back to Tessa, the vampress said, "There is no way I'll be able to sleep."

Deeya wrapped her arms around Tessa again. Tessa pressed her face into Deeya soft bosom. Then she heard the song. She knew exactly what song it was. She wanted to protest, but she knew she needed what was coming. They both needed their strength.

Tessa went limp in Deeya's arms and Deeya caught her. She picked up the beautiful naked woman and carried her to bed. She gently laid her into the soft warmth of the plush sheets, went to retrieve the thick cover, crawled into bed, wrapped her arms around the sleeping woman, pulled her close, and fell asleep with her. Not even the sound of the servant delivering the food woke the pair as they slept for a few hours of the day.....

Movement 5: To Dance with a Demon

Deeya had discovered, at a very young age that elves were different than most other species and needed very little, if any, sleep. When she learned meditation during her stay at a monastery after her dark years, she found that just meditating for a handful of hours would give her the rest she needed each day. When inside meditation, she found that she could focus on music: imagine the words, notes, and songs; be able to see them all form before her eyes, and transform all things musical into magical spells.

But on this day, with Tessa, she simply slept. If Tessa was even close to right, she would be in a battle for her own life within a few hours. She awoke with Tessa curled against her, even though she was cold to the touch, her weight was grounding. There was strength beneath that stillness, and a kind of fragile trust in the way she pressed close. For the first time since coming to the Darkened Deal, Deeya wasn't just thinking about the nakedness of the woman next to her, but of the women she had let go of. Deeya's mind wandered to memories of the two Tessa had mentioned before. The wolf-girl and the mage....

Deeya let go of Tessa and moved to the foot of the bed. She crossed her legs, closed her eyes, and simply allowed herself to breath. Focus. Tessa's suite, which she had now spent so much time in suddenly became far clearer in her mind. From the relics scattered around to the textures of the cloths, the room was vibrant and alive. She found herself able to remember things clearly that she had only glanced at, like the figurine that she had been distracted away from so many hours ago.

Finally, she allowed herself to picture the book, the words in the book, and the musical spells themselves. She thought about the notes on the scale, how they sounded, reverberating in the air, how they would sound on a lute, and how they would sound if she sang them. She pictured certain notes attaching to her drawn arrows in her mind's eye as she sang them. They came out soundless and stuck to the focused object, an arrow in this case. The spell slowly leaked sound, notes falling off of the thin shaft as she held the arrow drawn back to her cheek. She then mentally released the arrow and imagined it flying away from her. The impact itself broke all the notes from the arrow and the sound simply exploded.

She went over it, again and again, focusing the song more, which allowed less notes to bleed from the shaft of the arrow as she refined the technique without actually having to perform it. In the back of her mind, though, she knew something was missing, something she needed to learn. What if she missed? She only carried three arrows attached to the sheath that held her curved elven sword, which had been strapped to her back before she partially disrobed to climb into bed. What if she missed? Would there be enough? How could she let more than three arrows fly before she had to lay down her bow and defend herself? How accurate would more than three be if she rushed through them? She needed something, but what? A way not to miss.…

She opened her eyes and blinked, allowing her elven eyes to adjust quickly to the lighting in the room. The sky lights in the ceiling revealed that the sun was setting. Probably only an hour left before the Wolf's Moon crested the horizon. She scooted off the bed and bent over to get her clothes. "You are such a tease, Bard."

She tried to calm herself, keeping her movements careful, not wanting to give Tessa any more excuses for commentary. "You are such a voyeur, Tessa."

Tessa smirked. "Bard, I notice everything. Especially when it's you. Especially when it's *that* view."

Deeya stood, holding her clothes, and smirked over her shoulder, "As long as you enjoy yourself."

"Oh, I most certainly am." The rustle of the sheets said more than words, and Deeya didn't comment further.

Deeya then redressed herself, making sure everything was in place. Tessa remained sprawled in the sheets, not hiding the sounds she made. Slow, unhurried, unashamed. Deeya tried to focus, even as her ears burned. It was hard not to be amazed at how overtly sexual the woman truly was. As sexual as most bards were, Deeya would sometimes find herself wondering why she had such feelings about sex, but then the memories of her first love would come crashing back. Those scars would reopen, and her sexuality would retreat further into herself.

Most of her species, the elves that lived in the forest along with the Fae, were free with their nudity, being closer to nature, when around their own kind. There was no real immodesty among them as their natural bodies were not a taboo. But, like their urban cousins, when they needed to present themselves, they would adorn themselves in the most amazing form of dress. The urban elves, though, were overly modest, barely any of their flesh ever showed, but the woodland elves showed quite a bit, but in a beautiful, very artistic way.

Deeya had been raised among humans and dwarves, cultures where modesty was more about protection than beauty, less what you wore, more what you didn't reveal. The bard that had trained her in her youth taught her that even the drab clothing of the refugees could be used to great effect. On stage she learned that showing a little skin was part of the show, and the more you left to the imagination the better. But still, Deeya's past made her out of touch with most societal norms, but that made her unique, with a style all her own, with a modesty all her own.

Tessa arose from the bed and stretched. Deeya watched her and when Tessa was done, and noticed that Deeya had actually watched her, which made Tessa blush, but not in a demure way. Before she could start the game and point it out Deeya said, "How do we go about this? When do we get started?"

Tessa looked at the skylight and sighed. "I'm sure you have a clue about how much I dread this...."

"I'm sure you do every month, but come win or lose, this will be the last time."

Tessa looked into Deeya's sharp green eyes, set with resolve to get the mission done. It was part of Deeya that Tessa had known was there, but never fully believed. Sure, she knew that Deeya was more than just a bard, she found the best information, got into the most exclusive places, but did Deeya work only for herself, or was there a purpose to her making herself famous? Bards were more of a happy-go-lucky sort, drifting around, doing whatever they could to get by, yet Deeya never seemed to want for money, but if she had money, why was she living the lifestyle of one of the most pauperesque professions?

Determination, it leaked into Tessa, it was infectious. If bards could only be one thing, they were inspiring. Deeya inspired Tessa greatly in that moment. With determination in her voice Tessa said, "Yes, this will be the last time."

Deeya and Tessa sat, and without any more of the game, worked through their plan a few more times slightly partaking of the food that had been brought. Deeya scanned through the bardic book, hoping to find something that would help her not miss, for if she did, all three people involved, including herself, would likely die horribly, though she did not share her concerns with Tessa....

Tessa gave them a small amount more time after the moon had crested the horizon. She knew that if she looked too eager that the demon would know something was up. It was during that time that Tessa said, "You have never asked what I plan to give you in compensation for doing this."

Deeya looked up from the book, seeing past Tessa's naked body, looking into her blue eyes, and said, "You have always paid me generously for anything I've ever done for you. I expect you know what you are asking, and are prepared to give more than what you think is fair."

Tessa smirked. "Deeya, I'm a swindler, I always have been, no matter how I've treated you in the past."

Deeya grinned back at her smirk, "True, but something tells me you would never treat a friend poorly, unless you had to." As she said the comment, she remembered again that this stunning beauty in front of her was a vampire. The stories always told of seduction and murder. Would she be the same without the demon's leash?

"Fine, I'll offer you my body for this!"

Both women laughed wholeheartedly. The last laugh before the deed was to be done. And once the laugh was completed, Tessa strode forward and kissed Deeya. It was in her eyes, she could not help it, she absolutely had to. It was not some romantic toe-curling kiss, nor was it a sloppy kiss full of passion, it was just a simple, hard kiss. Deeya allowed it to happen, no resisting, and even kissed her back in the slightest of ways.

Tessa ended the kiss, pressed her forehead against Deeya's, and whispered "Sorry about that, I absolutely needed that."

Deeya grinned, "No one should ever be denied a last kiss."

Tessa pushed away from Deeya and said, "Let's get this done." She took a few steps and stopped, she then turned quickly, making her breasts sway seductively. "I thought you were going to bring a bow."

Deeya reached on the left side of her belt and unclipped a small metallic box. The box was made out of a green looking metal, with lines all around it. It was small, so small Tessa could not figure out what might be inside it. Then the bard did something.... It started making sounds, like a series of clicks. A string dropped out of it and the box opened, then opened again, then opened again.... Within seconds Deeya was holding a full size short, recurve bow, made out of metal and segregated into pieces the size of the box

Tessa stood open-mouthed, a rare moment of silence clashing strangely with her usual naked confidence. For once, she was caught off guard. "What in the...what kind of magic was that?"

Deeya grinned, "Not magic at all." Tessa looked at Deeya for more explanation. "I'm sure you heard about the debris that fell along with the sky in the Destroyed Lands, the event that trapped me there as an infant?"

Tessa frowned and nodded, Deeya continued, "Well, people have been reverse engineering it, making all manner of gadgets." Deeya held up the bow, "This is just one of mine."

Tessa put her hands on her nude hips and said, "Bard, inspiration, hero, tease, musical sorceress, and now engineer?"

Deeya shrugged, "Most people call this tinkering."

Tessa then grabbed Deeya's shirt, right between her breasts, and said, "If you don't stop impressing me, I'm going to take out my craving on you without your consent, this darkened deal the demon dealt me be damned."

Deeya blinked as her mind raced. "Darkened Deal," she said out loud, pushing the humorous amount of d-words out of her head. "The name for the inn is an inside joke to the demon's deal?"

Tessa smirked, pulling the bard close to her, her fist still entwined in the bard's shirt, "Someone finally got it."

Deeya lolled her head back and giggled. "The Deal now has the best name I have ever heard."

Tessa giggled as well, dropping Deeya from her clutches. "It is good is it not?"

Deeya adjusted her shirt, smoothing the fabric where Tessa had grabbed her. "Gods, woman, naming your prison after the crime is genius."

Tessa smiled sadly, "Hopefully I won't have to change it if we live."

The bard put her fist, which held her bow, against Tessa's sternum. The location was intimate, but Deeya ignored the woman's obvious nudity and locked her gaze into Tessa's eyes. "Don't you dare change it."

Tessa's smile changed from sad to rueful as she said laid her hand on Deeya's green, metallic vambrace. "Deal," she said with a wink.

Deeya dropped her fist and closed her eyes to giggle. "Why did you have to point this joke out to me now...if I giggle as we are getting ripped apart by giant spiders, you better remember you caused it."

Tessa's smile became a smirk. She then stroked Deeya's cheek as sadness flashed behind her eyes. "Come on bard, let us finish this."

The two women, elf and vampire, entered the cave through the wardrobe. The pair walked in silence and Deeya noticed, in the light of her magical orb, that Tessa seemed to be touching the walls as they went. The gesture seemed to be almost nostalgic in a way. She found it interesting how easily her attention stayed on the path ahead this time around. The determination and power that Tessa wielded should have been distracting enough to draw her eye. Deeya pondered over the thought of being with someone so much that you become used to the nakedness of their body. Her mind drifted to the two women whom with she had shared her body, Alou's dark chocolate skin, Ash's alabaster, lithe body.

Deeya took a deep breath and banished the women from her mind. It was time to focus. It was time to ready herself for war. It was time to prepare for death.

Tessa kissed her own hand and placed it against the glass-like tomb of her beloved as they walked by. When they got a few steps past his tomb, she said, "It starts here, Bard, vanish now, and do your best."

Deeya let Tessa get a few more steps away, allowed the orb dissipate completely, and started humming an entirely different tune softly to herself. Her eyes adjusted to the near pitch blackness, due to her being an elf, and due to a soft red light coming from the passageway in front of them. Tessa never turned to look back, but if she had, even in the brightest of days, Deeya's form would have been nothing but a shimmer.

Deeya watched Tessa make the corner and head into the red glow of the chamber beyond. When Deeya reached the turn, herself, she instinctively stayed close to the wall so as to minimize the chance of her being spotted. The rock itself, which lined the chamber, seemed to be emanating the glow. The large cavern held an immensely eerie feeling, with walls and ceiling that glowed red like blood. There were webbings from spiders hanging all over the place, but none seemed to take away from the deep red, which even the rocky floor seemed to produce. Tessa had strode out to the middle of the cavern. Her pale form bathed in the deep red light looked almost ritualistic, as if the glow twisted something sacred into something profane.

She raised her arms and said, "Oh great one, I come here in nothing but my skin, offering myself in accordance with our pact. My body and my power are given willingly to your greatness so that you might achieve a power beyond those who are wrong in thinking they out match your wonder."

Tessa's voice did not sound very convincing, but the words, themselves, almost made Deeya blurt out loud, "You have to be fucking kidding me." But she said nothing. She continued her soft hum as she strode softly into the chamber itself as her eyes darted around the area looking for signs of life. She did not venture far past the entrance, as she waited for the humiliating line to bring the demon into view.

When it moved Deeya realized it had been in view the whole time. Against the far wall sat a lump of what Deeya thought was just more rock formations, but it was, in fact, a morbidly obese spider. The disgusting sight was almost impossible to describe in her mind, as these eight spindly legs moved extruded themselves from folds in the voluminous skin which seemed nothing more than a lumpy formation on the rocky cavern floor. The bulbous, misshapen head was almost human, except for the fact that it had mandibles for a mouth and three black beady eyes where each normal eye should have been. It had two other eyes around where its ears should have been. All the eyes were bulbous, black orbs....

And then it spoke, the voice reverberating around the cavern, almost as if the sound of it speaking was coming from the walls themselves. "You come late, as always. Fortunate, as you will again be punished by me cumming late as well."

The cavern was probably fifty yards across and Deeya had a clear shot, but she remembered the plan. The demon had to be distracted by sex. In her mind, Deeya knew that this was something she did not want to see. She almost entered meditation as she steeled herself for what was to come.

Tessa, continuing to hold her hands up like she was on display, said, "My body is yours for your pleasure, as you sustain me, give me life. I come before you to honor my end of the agreement in good faith, as you have so done."

Deeya was finding it near impossible to keep still and silent, for even she heard the unspoken words between the halfhearted, poorly worded statement that Tessa was forced to relate. Those words between words could be heard in the tone Tessa had, cursing the twisted agreement, the darkened deal, as it were. Deeya held on to the inside joke, trying to find inspiration from the sadistic mirth of it to keep her hand's fingers from taking the arrows that were now in her hand, nocking one, and letting it fly. Luckily, if one could use that word for such situations, the bard had been in other situations where patience was the key, waiting for the perfect moment to land the perfect strike.

The demon's voice reverberated triumphantly throughout the cavern, an ominously demonic sound. "Then come forth and service me like the whore you are."

Tessa then started walking, far too slowly for Deeya's tastes, but then, she had probably been coached to do so, over and over again. It hit Deeya right then, twelve months a year, for over a thousand years…. Maybe even two thousand years. Over and over again…. This event she was witnessing….

The spindly legs reached out for Tessa. Her gasp echoed off the eerie red cavern walls, as she was lifted off her feet. It was pure horror to Deeya's eyes. Unceremoniously Tessa was turned, her arms were held apart, her legs were spread, and…a brown, wormlike thing extended upwards from below. The demon handled her like an object, lifting and twisting her with its limbs.

And then the final appendage inserted….

Tessa's body was rocked by the insertion and her gasp tore through the chamber. Sharp, pained, and hollow. She writhed as the demon continued, and every sound that followed was agony.

But the demon, he was enjoying himself. It almost sounded as if he was slobbering as its spindly limbs caressed the helpless woman in revolting delight. Its words, if they were words, were unintelligible.

Deeya pushed back the urge to violently vomit by resolving to end this...this abomination. She could almost clearly see the demon's near human face behind Tessa. It would be a tight shot, but it was time to take it. Deeya took two more steps forward, hoping to give herself more than the inch she had, while she maneuvered the arrows in her right hand. She brought her right hand to the string of the bow, nocking her first arrow. The other two arrows hung down from the tight grip she had on them with her pinky and ring fingers. The metallic string drew fluidly, as she raised the bow to take aim down the shaft that went from her two fingers on the string to her other finger, holding the bow. As she leveled the bow and drew the arrow ever closer, she took a deep breath, and the invisibility faded away. Forming the words in her mind, the notes in her mouth, she thought about how exactly to sing the song. The arrow finally reached her cheek. Deeya felt the cold metal string, the rough wood of the arrow shaft, the tickle of the green colored hawk feathers. Her string and lungs had been drawn to their peak tautness. Her mind knew the sequence, release one, then the other. She let go a blood curdling scream, in the perfect keys, yet no sound was heard.

The demon had seen the bard the instant the invisibility dropped. It started a sentence. "What...." The first word started to reverberate around the room, a loud cacophony that only just reached Deeya's ears the exact moment she released the sound engorged arrow. And in that exact moment she had an idea, but it was far too late for the first arrow, as it sped quickly away from her.

As the demon said, "is…" the arrow attempted to navigate the tiny space between Tessa's arm and face, but the demon had already started to move Tessa to block the arrow in flight. It gashed Tessa's cheek, down to the bone, and veered wildly off course.

Before the first arrow had even finished cutting its way through Tessa's skin, Deeya was drawing back another. This time, she knew exactly what to do. She repeated the pattern, deep breath, tickle of the feather against the cheek, shrill; violent; soundless scream directly into the second arrow, and as soon as her lungs were empty, she inhaled again and pursed her lips, almost as if she was going to whistle.

The demon finished its question with the word, "this?" As the demon's second word reached the bard's ear, though, Deeya released the second arrow. Tessa was starting to yell in pain as blood squirted from the fresh, deep gash in her cheek and a section of hair that had gotten in the way of the arrow, fell away from her head, starting its slow descent towards the cavern floor. The demon attempted to pull his long…*thing* out of her, though it was pinned inside her, as her own orgasm gripped it tightly. With a spasmed pull, the grotesque appendage tore free from her body. Her breath choked off into a ragged scream.

The first arrow thudded into the wall behind the demon and simply exploded. The shrill sound of Deeya whistling, though, was evident before the concussion wave tore a chunk out of the wall, reflecting back towards the demon's head. The whistle almost drowned out the sound of the bow string thwapping as Deeya released the arrow. Oddly, though, Deeya had aimed far to the right, a shot that was obviously going to miss the demon and Tessa altogether.... It seemed a gross overcompensation, as the first arrow had just barely missed to the left.

But then...something strange happened.... The arrow, seemingly listening to Deeya's whistle, turned just as Deeya changed the notes. It made a hard left going around Tessa by a large margin. The demon, being blown forward by the concussion wave from the first exploding arrow was pushed towards the second arrow, catching it directly in the neck.

As soon as the arrow found its mark, Deeya had already knocked the third and final arrow and was starting to pull it backwards. The explosion turned the revolting scene into something straight out of nightmares, as a very large amount of blood expanded outwards with the soundwave. The arrow itself had sunk in almost to its fletching before it exploded. Both concussion waves reached Tessa as the bowstring reached Deeya's cheek. Deeya started to scream again as Tessa was torn out of the demon's legs on a wave of blood and started her trajectory across the cavern. As Tessa was moved out of the way, Deeya got to see the destruction her second arrow had caused. It looked like a wall of blood, as it fountained out of the obese, disgusting, demonic spider's body.

It was then that she noticed, something else coming out of the ruined demon beside blood. She saw the black spindly legs that were clawing their way out of the abdomen of the beast. Was the demon pregnant with its own minions? Deeya did not give the question any more thought. The wave of blood splattered against the ceiling of the cavern and had pushed out enough that there was plenty of space amongst the droplets, the moment she had been waiting for....

Deeya pursed her lips again and released. As she did, the soundwave of the explosions hit her, but she kept whistling. The arrow did not need to hear the directions, for they were magic, not sound. The sound of the whistle was nothing more than something akin to the words that cast the spell. The arrow dodged and weaved, righting itself as it rode the shockwaves of sound, continuing on its perfect trajectory to the gaping hole where the demon's neck had been attached to the front part of its body. At the last possible moment, Deeya's whistle changed notes and the arrow dipped, striking the demon dead center of what Deeya figured was the creature's chest.

Even though her eyes had been locked onto the arrow and its target while she had been flying through the air, she did not get to see the resulting force from the explosion as major chunks of demon's flesh flew through the air, as she landed hard in the cavern hallway she had originally entered the cavern from. Having been concentrating more on the arrow than her own preservation, she landed awkwardly, on her rear. She knew from the depth of the pain that a sizable bruise would blossom there before the spiders would tear her apart.

She heard the bow skitter away from her, the metal bouncing off of the rock of the cave along with the sounds she had been fearing she would hear. An echoing of otherworldly sounds emanated from the cavern system back the way they had entered from. The chittering and squealing could have only come out of a child's arachnophobic nightmares. The repulsive sound was the battle cry of a horde of giant spiders coming to join the newly excreted ones that were rushing towards the bard.

Tessa slammed into the wall a few feet to the left of Deeya and the mouth of the cave, with a sickening thud, and after that, she fell limply to the ground, seemingly unconscious. As Deeya started to stand, to ready herself for what was to come. The wave of blood hit the cavern wall, sounding like a wave against a shore. Deeya was getting to her feet deep enough into the hallway-like entrance that she got no blood on her at all.

Deeya finished standing, unsheathed her sword with her left hand, unholstered the axe with her right, and forgot all about her bow. She hummed a song, which made the blade of her axe glow with its own inner magical light, and ran back into the glowing red cavern again where she was met head on with the medium-dog sized spiders that were rushing towards her. The first one leapt high into the air, obviously planning on falling upon Deeya with all its considerable weight. Deeya yelled at it, a single loud note escaping her mouth. The spider was thrown further upwards and backwards, being killed by the soundwave, landing amongst the twenty or thirty some odd spiders behind it.

At this point, Deeya no longer saw anything outside of the next twenty or thirty things she had to kill to stay alive. The middle section of the demon lay open, a bloody heart beat slowly within the ruined cavity. The sickly black heart of a demon. As long as that particular organ continued beating, the demon would repair itself, and come back with a vengeance. But Deeya had no more arrows, no more bow, and her only thoughts and movements were bent on slashing, weaving, screaming, hacking, kicking, punching, singing, spinning, cutting, and anything else she had to add to her dance. And it was a dance. She danced the dance because her life depended on it. She danced, graceful and deadly. She danced with death inside a cave underneath the pale moon light of the Wolf's Moon she could not even see. She did not even notice when the horde of spiders poured out of the cave entrance behind her, swarming her, as she had already been surrounded. Her every breath and movement was bent on killing, and that murderous determination was simply called survival.

Throughout her dance, Deeya never saw Tessa get to her feet. Deeya never saw Tessa's naked, blood drenched body move, though wobbly, in full sprint towards the ruin of bloody flesh and gore that was the body of the demon as she danced. Deeya did not see Tessa struggle to climb the corpse of the demon. Deeya never saw the fangs that Tessa bared, as her jaw unhinged in a violently horrifying manor. And Deeya definitely did not see the vampire bite into the demon's heart, which stood half as tall as her naked human form, nor did she see the vampire get coated in a fountain of blood as the heart simply popped like a blister.

Instead, Deeya danced. She danced and killed to survive. Suddenly, without warning, her present tense form of "survive" became "survived." Past tense. It took the Emerald Bard seven steps of the dance, two yells, and three strikes through the empty air to bring the dance to a halt, as all the spiders stopped rushing.

Deeya was coated with a glistening sheen of sweat. She looked around her for just a moment to realize the spiders were no longer attacking, before she fell to her hands and knees to the cavern floor. The floor around her was barren of blood due to all the concussion waves she had pushed forth. In fact, the stone floor was probably cleaner than it had ever been.

Deeya was panting so hard, the sound of which was echoing around the cavern, that she did not hear Tessa approaching her. When Tessa entered the cleared circle around Deeya, though, the bard moved as fast as lightning. She spun around wildly, but her sword stopped as it touched the skin of Tessa's neck.

Tessa, herself, was near unrecognizable. Her skin was covered in thick, red blood, spotted with chunks of gore. It oozed off of her, dripping in thick droplets. She looked like a demon goddess, birthed from death, painted in the blood of the demon, with her hair slicked back as if she was ascending from a baptism. Deeya blinked at her, breathing so heavily she could hardly speak. She managed to say, "Tessa?"

Tessa grinned, her seductive grin looking so menacingly evil, underneath her layer of oozing blood. "We did it, Bard."

Deeya looked around at the spiders. Many were still alive, but all were hanging back from her, as if watching her. Deeya managed to say, "The spiders?"

Tessa said, "Under my control."

Deeya turned back to gaze into Tessa's eyes, the edge of her sword was still touching the skin of Tessa's neck as the blood that coated the woman slowly oozed onto it. She looked deep into Tessa's eyes. She had one last question, the most important question her mind had ever known. Breathlessly she said, "And you?"

Tessa laughed, not moving from Deeya's blade, and said, "Me? I'm still me, well, maybe more me than I...." She cut herself off and looked down the cavern, her expression revealing a fair amount of shock. Then she exclaimed, "He's awake!"

Movement 6: A Light in the Dark

Tessa shoved Deeya's sword aside and took off at a dead run. Deeya watched the spiders make room for her to go, giving her plenty of room. Deeya took no chances, she took a deep breath and started a simple song. The first words were, "Ohhhhh, the road is long," and suddenly all time as she normally perceived it slowed down around her. She took off at a run and the world itself turned into a blur. She quickly caught up with Tessa, overtook her, and made it to the glass-like frozen waterfall. Upon arriving she started another song, singing the word, "burn," in a scale like pattern. Suddenly, all the long dormant torches in the room sprang to life.

The light from all the small fires reflected off the frozen glass-like, almost mirror-like, ceiling and the entire cavern, smaller yet taller than the one that held the demon, became shockingly illuminated in bluish-white light. Deeya found herself suddenly beyond tired again. She fell to her knees for the second time, panting.

Tessa stopped running as she entered the room. She gawked at the bard and said, "Deeya, you are amazing."

Deeya then looked at the waterfall itself. It was a single pillar in the middle of the room, reaching all the way up to the ceiling. Tiny droplets of water were streaming down the surface as it was starting to melt. As Tessa strode towards it, more and more water started to slough down the column, clinging to the surface, disappearing into the floor of the cavern. Deeya rose up and sat on her heels, her back straightening as she studied the column of water that was coming to life before her eyes. She also took a good look at Tessa.

The vampress's blood-soaked form was stark against the bluish-white of the room. She looked like a revenant, reborn through violence and victory. The blood clung to her every curve, dripping from her in clinging droplets. It clung to her like a second skin.

She stood next to Deeya and smiled down at the sweat covered, physically exhausted bard. She stepped closer, her blood-slick hand reached out as she said, "Here, let me help."

Deeya fought the urge to step back. Her reaction was automatic, she always hated to be touched without consent, whether it be by the horrific visage of a blood soaked vampress or not. She felt the dampness of Tessa's blood-soaked right palm press against her upper chest and suppressed a shudder.

Tessa whispered, "From my soul, to yours." Deeya's breath simply caught. It scared her, she could not breathe at all. Her eyes widened, but she felt something else besides terror. She felt life. Invigorating, renewing life. After Tessa took a few breaths herself, she smiled and removed her hand. As she did, Deeya could feel the tacky goo tug against her skin, leaving behind a bloody handprint, along with a strange mixture of renewal and repulsion.

As soon as the contact was over, Deeya was able to breathe again. She stood straight up as the breath rushed in, arching her back as her body spasmed. As she breathed out, though, her entire body relaxed and all her pain, tiredness, soreness, and stress went with the air.

Tessa smiled at the standing bard. "Welcome back, Bard."

Deeya smiled, though she figured she looked silly with a dark red handprint on her chest. "I'm surprised that didn't come with a kiss."

Tessa laughed, "Oh, that's the next level of healing that can heal the almost dead. And yes, before you ask, there is a third, which can actually bring people back to life." Tessa then looked beyond Deeya, to the pillar that was almost pure liquid again, "But honestly, Bard, my next kiss belongs to someone else."

She reached into the water and found her lover's chest. She did not need to say any words, as he was fully healed. He had been the entire time he had been encased within the healing waters that had frozen around him. Then, thick arms and large hands reached out of that formally frozen water, grabbed the full-fledged, blood soaked vampire, and pulled her into the pillar of flowing liquid. For a moment, the entire column of water turned red, as the blood was washed off of Tessa. For another moment, it seemed like the entire room turned from a bluish-white to blood red. It had an eerie effect, like something changed within the entire structure itself.

Deeya took the time to finally sheath her sword and holster the axe when the room turned back to bluish-white. She spent the few moments she had alone reflecting over her survival and the feel of the wet handprint as the blood dried on her chest. The two figures within the water writhed together for a length of time before they finally stepped out.

They came forth from the cascading water like artwork of ancient gods and goddesses, regal and reborn. Their naked forms reminiscent of perfect statues from the most prominent museums and art galleries of the world.

Silus was tall, muscular, and moved like a cat. His wet silver hair hung down his back swinging limply like his spent phallus, which still had the flush of blood from having been used. Even flaccid, his manhood was obscenely large. Like Tessa, his form seemed to be designed off of someone's over the top sexual fantasy.

They had their hands intertwined. He stepped down first and smiled at Deeya. Deeya looked up at his face, then followed it downward, as he knelt in front of her. "It seems I owe you my life."

Tessa groaned, "Always the showman."

Silus turned his head slightly and smirked back over his shoulder at her. "In our day, bards were the ones with the flair for the dramatic." He then turned his deep, penetrating gaze back to Deeya. He took her hand and said, "And it was only customary to show them respect in their own way." He then kissed Deeya's hand, tenderly, softly, even reverently, that Deeya reluctantly allowed. After he was done, he touched the back of her hand to his forehead and said, "From this moment forth, know that I will honor you with my every breath, for I owe all the ones from now until my death, to you."

Deeya had seen this custom before, but only in the urban elves, who called themselves high-elves. They were normally tall, majestic creatures with porcelain skin and silver or blonde hair, and every single one of them carried themselves higher than anyone else. They were immortal and believed they should be the aristocracy of the world. Sure, it made them seem like pompous asses, but it was their way.

When the kneeling vampire, whose body as well as words reminded her of those urban elves, finished his sacred vow to her, she placed her other hand, her left hand, on the top of his head and said, "Arise, one who has pledged his intent and hear my will."

He looked up at her in a type of shock, then shared a glance with Tessa. She shrugged, the movement making her now washed-clean body shift like a figure in a dream. "I told you, she is a special breed."

Deeya realized it, right then. The two shared a mental bond, they could hear each other's thoughts somehow. Deeya had heard of stories where people were so much in love, they could do such a thing, or they had a spell cast on them that allowed it. Either way, it made her smile, as she was responsible for these two being unleashed from their respective prisons, it was good to have more awareness of their abilities.

He stood up, tall before her. When he finished standing, Deeya said, "You are to love Tessa, wholeheartedly until the day your breath stops for good.

You are to live your life within your morals. And you are to live said life with a song in your heart, as music resonates within us all."

He grinned, "Thank you, milady. I will do thusly, and more, as you are not getting out of my thanks so easily."

Deeya laughed and placed a hand on his arm, above his elbow. It felt as though she had put her hand on solid, carved granite. Feeling his skin, though, cool under her touch, soft over the hard, made her realize that his manhood was directly in front of her, just within her lower peripheral vision. She then said, "I expected as much. So, from here on out, let us call ourselves, at the very least, friends."

He grinned down at her and clasped her arm. She was quick to pull away. But the light touch still surprised him greatly, as he felt strength beneath the shirt. The bard was no soft poet, she was forged, like him, through a life lived. Most of the bards he had known in his time had been soft. It made him also realize that his manhood was directly in front of her, which made it stir a little. "I hope we can be more than friends."

Tessa seemed to change her expression, like she was thinking something. He then snapped his head towards her and shrugged. Deeya dropped her hand, rolled her eyes, and dramatically said, "Not you, too!"

Silus turned toward the bard and held his hands up saying, "What did I do?"

Tessa then laughed and said, "Get over it, Bard, you are highly fuckable."

Deeya's eyes bugged a bit, before she closed her eyes and shook her head while taking a deep breath with her hands on her hips.

Silus looked at Tessa who then sighed and said, "I'm sorry Deeya, I mean you are incredibly beautiful, in an irresistible way."

Deeya then squinted her eyes at Silus, "Wait, you're the one that keeps her in line?"

Silus grinned and shrugged while saying, "I do what I can."

Deeya then asked, "So, was she always this bad?"

Silus replied, "All of our kind were, especially the aristocracy. Oh, the orgies that I had to attend, serving drink...."

Tessa actually looked shocked, "I didn't hear you complaining when some of us would break off and come back to our rooms."

"Of course not. Do you remember Shanice?" Tessa nodded and he continued, "It was the only time I could get inside her, when she was kissing on you."

Deeya finally said, "Whoa, wait, seriously, you two go back to talking telepathically, this is too much information to be thrown about in the open."

Both of them had the audacity to look shocked, as if they did not believe Deeya would have ever found out. Deeya then continued, "And seriously, you two are naked, in a cold damp cavern, there are demon spawn spiders right there in that entry way," Deeya even pointed to them, "and my bow is on the far side of them...."

Silus frowned and Tessa looked towards the spiders. "Sorry, Bard, it will take me some time to understand how to command them well."

Silus said, "So that memory you gave me wasn't just a dream?"

Tessa shook her head, "No, I have claimed the demon's powers as my own. I control his spawn, though I don't think I can make any more, and we'll never have to feed again when we are here, in our home."

Silus looked distant for a moment, as his eyes unfocused and he looked well beyond the wall above Deeya's head. He whispered, "A life without the taste of blood," as if he could not believe it were possible.

Deeya heard movement behind her, towards the entrance she had pointed to, with the spiders. She turned her body away from the nude man and looked at the spiders, themselves. One of the smaller spiders, walked into the room on six legs, the other two were holding her bow. Deeya had never been a spider person, she killed them every chance she got, but as this one, as large as a wolf, stopped in front of her, raising up her bow for her, she saw it as some form of dog, a tame animal trying to please its master. Deeya took the bow and it skittered off to the cave with the rest of the spiders, then in almost unison, the spiders all turned and retreated down the tunnel together.

Silus then said, "That is damnable creepy...."

Tessa laughed, running her hands through her damp hair before saying, "Yeah, but we'll get used to it." She then sighed, "Deeya has a point, though, let's go up and get dry and warm."

As Tessa's hair fell back down around her face, the missing hair was quite obvious. Silus said, "That could become a new style."

Tessa felt the short locks, how they rested against her completely healed cheek, "Maybe. Though it will probably be more of an annoyance than anything else."

As they started walking towards the way back to the inn, Deeya said, "Yeah, sorry about that, he moved you faster than I anticipated he would."

Tessa laughed, "Do not worry." She then took and squeezed Deeya's hand, "It was only pain, besides it already healed and we are alive."

Deeya squeezed Tessa's hand in return and said, "Amen."

Tessa looked into Deeya's eyes and said, "Amen indeed, Bard, amen indeed." Tessa's eyes narrowed as she seemed to remember something, "Did I see that second arrow you shot turn in some way?"

Deeya shrugged, "It landed where I wanted it to."

After sharing a laugh, they walked in silence for a bit. Silus and Deeya let Tessa lead the way, though it was probably because Silus wanted to watch Tessa's rear swaying. As they reached the stairs, Silus said, "So it was obvious, about our mental link?"

Deeya nodded, "Yeah. So you can share memories?"

Silus laughed, "In a way. It just kind of happens when we make love."

Tessa laughed, not turning around as they ascended the stairs. "Most wouldn't call it love, the kind of sex we have."

Silus smiled at her nude rear end that was wagging practically in front of his face. It was more in front of Deeya's face, but as he was next to her.... He reached out and grabbed it, saying, "We know. You call it 'hard fucking.' Even the sensual passionate kind we share." He then smiled at Deeya, while feeling the muscles of her rear work to propel her up the stairs, "How can you resist this, Deeya?"

Deeya smirked, even though Tessa was holding her hips in such a way that both she and Silus had a clear view of Tessa's female anatomy. Deeya tried not to look at it, though it was right there, as she said, "Well, as hard as she made it to resist, I crave something far more than the carnal when I share myself with someone."

Silus nodded, letting go of Tessa's rear. "Go on," he urged.

Deeya shrugged, "I don't know what to say other than that." She sucked on her lower lip, thinking about the best sexual experiences she had, and what made them special. "I just need more of a spiritual connection. When I'm with someone, I want to experience their soul, and have them experience mine."

Tessa stepped through the wardrobe and into her suite. Silus motioned for Deeya to go first. He then ducked through and said, "And that is what I share with Tessa. No matter what she wants to call it, I feel that when I'm with her, in whatever capacity, I truly experience her love for me." He reached out and took Tessa's hand, "And I hope she experiences mine for her."

Tessa grinned carnally. She shook off his hand and reached down to grab his cock, "Oh, I experience something all right."

Deeya rolled her eyes dramatically and shook her head before she started walking towards the door. Before she could say goodbye to the couple, Tessa jogged up to her and put a hand on her shoulder. "Deeya," she whispered.

Deeya stopped and turned to look into Tessa's eyes. Tessa grinned demurely, which looked odd with her sultry good looks. When her eyes looked into Deeya's. Her gaze was deep and serious as she said, "Deeya, honestly, I cannot possibly begin to thank you for this kindness."

Deeya smiled back to Tessa, "Tess, honestly, you don't have to thank...." Deeya's breath caught as Tessa kissed her for the second time. Like the first, it was unexpectedly warm, soft, and kind. Unlike the first time, though, Tessa's hands held Deeya's cheeks firmly. She had just held her lover's huge cock in one of those hands, yet she kissed Deeya with a tenderness that did not turn Deeya on at all. The kiss was not designed to. It was passionate, yet held no longing, just a little piece of tenderness between two who had faced a demon, together, and somehow lived its extermination.

Deeya did not pull back, she was allowing Tessa this one thing, after all the seduction and nudity, the begging and the pleading. They had both survived, why not allow the grateful friend something to remember her by? When Deeya did not pull back, Tessa pushed her hands back through Deeya's short hair, intertwining her fingers behind Deeya's head, bringing an intense sensuality to the now passionate gesture.

Tessa finished the kiss, which left both women rather breathless, and placed her forehead against

Deeya's. Both women opened their eyes and peered into each other's souls. Then...something changed. Tessa's eyes looked as though they had changed color, to a wolf like yellow. She then spoke in an odd accent, "A letter shall arrive for you here, on the morrow. This vessel will give it to you personally. If you open it, you will be set upon a journey that will intertwine your fate with the fate of all existence."

Deeya blinked, unmoving, watching those yellow eyes, which suddenly turned back to blue. Tessa smiled, and in her normal voice she said, "Sorry about that, I only wanted to thank you.... Tell you some things, some of the small things I was going to give you from the inn, free food, free stays.... I honestly did not mean to kiss you like that."

Deeya opened her mouth to speak but Silus said, "Do not worry much about that, Deeya, Tess has a gift of seeing important events in someone's future. The messages never tell if the choice laid before you is good or bad, or which choice is good or bad, only that a choice will be made, and it's more important than you will probably realize."

Deeya placed her hands on Tessa's forearms, which were on either side of Deeya's face, and said, "I understand, both of you. Tess, you have already thanked me, and I know that you will find ways to make sure I know how grateful you are, for a very long time."

Silus sniffed loudly. "If she ever stops," he said sarcastically.

Tessa smiled, used her hands to pull Deeya's head forward, and kissed Deeya's forehead. "I never knew my sisters, they all left the castle decades, if not centuries,

before I was born to my parents. I was their final child.
No one, I dare say not even family, if I had any, would
have risked their lives as much as you have for me,
Deeya. I have no kin, no relatives, and no family. But
now, I have a beautiful little bardic elf, who likes to wear
green, for family."

Silus strode forward, put a hand on Tessa's bare
shoulder, and said, "Deeya, she means every word, and
she's never said that to anyone. In fact, outside of the
staff, who are all bound to Tessa like minions, no one
living in the world knows about our vampirism. Just her
trusting you with that, and allowing you to keep that
secret and live, is a huge deal."

Tessa grinned, "Thank you, Deeya, and welcome to
the family."

Deeya grinned back at her, "No worries, and thank
you for trusting me, out of all the adventurers, so-called
heroes, and others that come through here."

Tessa gave Deeya's lips another chaste kiss, "Go
recuperate in your room, Deeya, the sun will be up soon.
Your letter should be here tomorrow morning. Perform
tonight and eat with us afterwards if you wish.
Tomorrow morning, I shall have a breakfast waiting for
you here in my suite. As you eat with us, the letter
should arrive, and you shall have it as soon as possible."

Tessa released Deeya's head and Deeya said,
"Alright, I shall see you later. I know you won't rest for
some time, but both of you at least *try* to recuperate as
well."

Tessa stopped Deeya from walking out the door.
"Go this way." She opened a secret door on the side of
the bed that was opposite the wardrobe entrance to the

cave system below the inn. "This leads to the closet next to the second-floor landing in the residential wing. Open the door, go up the stairs and you'll be at the suite level."

Tessa squeezed Deeya's hand before Deeya left the two vampires alone. The dark corridor would have been pitch black to a human, but to Deeya's elven eyes it was easily navigable. She followed Tessa's directions and found her way back to her room easily. Outside the windows she could see the light of dawn turning the horizon a stark pink. It was going to be a beautiful day, full of one less demon.

--

Back in Tessa's suite, the vampires talked for a long while. Just being amazed at hearing each other's voices. Silus was the first to bring up plans for the future. "We should create a small village here. A smithy for repairs would be a major boon for the travelers."

Tessa laughed lightly, enjoying laying her head on her lover's chest. No chest had ever equaled up to how perfect his was. "The simple idea of a future that we can plan...." She kissed his strong chest lightly to keep from tearing up. "I cannot believe we are free...."

Silus ran his fingers through his lover's hair, enjoying the feeling of touch, relishing it. "To think, a future.... In this village, we could have kids, or even capture an empire...."

Tessa smirked, "An empire, huh?"

He could sense her thoughts; she purposely avoided the idea of kids. "Well, your grandfather did it...."

Tessa laughed while looking into Silus's eyes. "Let us not fall into delusions of grandeur, just yet." She reached for his manhood with familiarity and reverence, her touch soft but confident as her smile grew. "Let us just enjoy what we've so missed...."

Silus struggled to control his breathing. Tessa had picked up so many new techniques, so many ways to give and receive pleasure that his mind could not cope with the glut of sensual memories. She massaged the limp phallus until it became an erection. Even though he had the memories, he was in no way prepared as the stunning beauty he loved so very much wrapped her mouth around his manhood. She moved her lips and tongue around slowly, gingerly enjoying the taste and texture of her lover's glorious organ. She even hummed from time to time, vibrating it in a way that sent sensations to other parts of his body.

Silus had always been the one in the partnership to last the longest, giving Tessa more than a few orgasms. But on this day, as Tessa's mouth released his cock, and she maneuvered to mount him, he found himself struggling not to prematurely explode. He had no clue about the difficulty of the task at hand, until her womanhood enveloped every inch of his aching phallus. He moaned and he writhed as he clenched his hands upon sheets, breasts, or ass. As she danced upon him, memories of her life flooded into him. There were a set of memories, though, that stood out above all else. Sad memories, of her masturbating herself to orgasm, spread wide in front of the column of ice. A tear formed in Tessa's eye at the same time as Silus's eye did the same.

In that moment, he sat up, braced Tessa's back, laid her back against the bed behind her, and sensually made love to her. As his lips kissed her neck and breasts her eyes filled with tears. For the first time, in longer than most civilizations have stood upon the world, Tessa cried. She cried for joy, she cried for sadness, and she cried because she was free. Free to love and free to live. And finally, it was time. Silus knew, because he could hear her thoughts. Their hands found each other's, their lips found each other's, and together, as their tears mingled upon Tessa's face, they experienced the same, soul warming orgasm. Tessa relished the feeling of his seed filling her up on the inside, as he collapsed against her, feeling her insides quiver against his spent manhood. The sex was beautiful, love-making passion. As daylight fell upon the world around them, the two vampric lovers explored sensuality, sexuality, and each other's bodies as well as their own; as they experimented with how to love each other again.

--

Meanwhile, Deeya had the servants bring her up some bath water and lit a fire under the copper tub. The luxury of another bath was not lost on her. She enjoyed the warm water in the silence of her room, especially after the blood washed off of her chest. She enjoyed sleeping in the silken sheets in nothing more than her own skin. She even enjoyed dressing up in her cleaned clothes and walked in the garden area behind the inn to reconnect with nature. As she made her way through garden trails down to one of the most dangerous rivers in the world. Deeya mused about how life itself continued forward, not knowing the dark secret that was below this area and how it would continue on long after one threat was dealt with. The demon, all the spiders, and now a pair of vampires. She let a leaf fall from her hand into the water of the swift flowing river and smiled at life itself.

As the sun started to set and she walked back to the inn, she knew she was going to perform for a while, just to think about the world, as she knew there was nothing more cathartic than just playing some music. She also knew that she was leaving on the following day. She had wanted her next trip to continue to the north, as she was hoping to catch a ship to Fo'Est, where her home was, yet she feared that this letter would send her elsewhere. Only time would tell.

The night went quickly, with requests coming in for her to sing certain songs, while most of it was spent simply playing ambient music with the lilting sounds of her lute. Afterwards she sat at the owner's table and ate with Tessa and Silus. After the hearty meal with pleasant conversation she retired to her room well after the halfway point of night had gone by.

Movement 7: A Letter Arrives

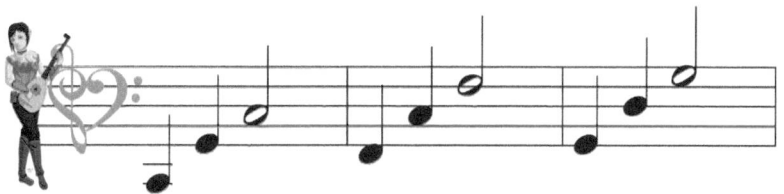

Deeya was deep within meditation when a knock came at the door. She had been dressed in her travel clothes since before her meditation, so she just got up and answered the door. A young blonde woman in servant's clothes stood at the door, her practiced expression betraying a quiet confidence. Her long braid rested over one shoulder, and her refined posture gave her an elegance that didn't match the uniform she wore. Her plump lips, eyeshadow, and blush had been painted with a dark, smoky style of makeup that really brought out her brown eyes. She was the type of girl that looked like she had money, even though she was wearing servant's clothes. Deeya imagined her in a formal gown and realized why someone might mistake her for nobility. The kind of beauty that changed people's decisions, for better or worse. Deeya thought she had run into most of the staff, but she did not recognize this young girl at all.

The girl was exactly Deeya's height, and she smiled at seeing Deeya, "I'm sorry to disturb you, but the mistress wanted me to make sure everything was okay and to see if you needed something before you came down for breakfast."

Deeya stood by the door, curious, as this seemed out of the ordinary. "No, everything is fine. When should I come down?"

The young woman looked down the hallway, like she was not wanting to be seen. When she looked back at Deeya she bit her very full lower lip and said, "May I come in?"

Deeya blinked at the request, and not knowing what to do, she simply stepped out of the way and let the woman in. She took the offer and stepped into the room. Deeya said, "Whatever is the matter?"

The girl turned to Deeya, as Deeya shut the door, and said, "Sorry, it's just, you know, impersonating the staff when they aren't expecting it, seems a bit wrong...."

Deeya did a quick mental check, making sure that her axe was at her side. Her sword, though, was lying next to her backpack at the head of the bed. "So...you're not staff?"

The girl gave Deeya a wry grin, a grin Deeya almost recognized from somewhere, "No, Deeya, I'm not staff.... Well, not technically."

Finally, it clicked. Deeya said, "Silus?"

The girl grinned, baring her teeth. "I was wondering if you would remember Tess telling you about my ability."

Deeya let out a breath she had not known she was holding. "Of course I remember."

Silus held her hands up and spun around, "So, what do you think?"

Deeya smiled. "Alluring and beautiful, as with most of the staff here."

Silus laughed. "This girl isn't on the staff, this is the one I was talking about, the one I always had a crush on, but only opened herself when she was with another woman."

Deeya thought, as she walked to the other side of the bed, "Shani, Chanty...."

Silus smiled at Deeya trying to remember the girl's name and said, "Good memory, Bard, but her name was Shanice."

Deeya smiled back at the young, pretty girl, and said, "She was quite a stunner."

Silus nodded sadly, sliding her hand across her chest to grab the braid and tug it. Deeya noticed the odd movement but realized that it was a man in a woman's body....

She then said, "I believed so as well." She sighed and sat on edge of the foot of the bed before continuing, "My entire life is so far into the past, no one I used to know is living, except Tessa. I got to experience her life, sure, but it has been lived within the prison she's become. She's changed so much, become harder...."

Deeya crawled up onto the bed and sat cross-legged towards Silus. After she settled, she said, "I'd be shocked if she hadn't, but I think I know what you mean. With her changing so much, you don't even know if you'd include her in those that you would claim to know."

Silus nodded sadly. She then did the same as Deeya, crawling up onto the bed and turning to face her, mirroring Deeya's posture, sitting cross-legged in her short dress without adjusting it. If she noticed what the pose revealed, she didn't show it.

"We are going to experiment with leaving, we should be able to be gone for weeks at a time, considering that's what the demon always said he did."

Deeya smiled and said, "That will be the best for both of you, a vacation, as it were." After a moment, Deeya asked, "Were you aware of time passing?"

Silus frowned and played with her braid while she thought, "After coming out of it, I can tell you that I was aware that time passed. It was like sleeping, you know when you wake up and know that you did not just close your eyes. You just know that time somehow had passed in between. I think I dreamed. I was not conscious. But I could tell, when I awoke, it had been a very long time."

"Probably for the best, a person's mind would have gone insane like that."

Silus's light brown eyes met Deeya's, "Very true, Bard, very true."

Deeya studied Silus's face during the silence that followed. It did not last overly long, but it was long enough to really get a feel for this soft, female face that looked so aristocratic and lovely. Finally, Deeya broke the silence, before it became awkward, and said, "Why did you come up here? Is it just to talk? Maybe ask me something?"

Silus turned red and looked down at her bare legs. "I'm sorry Deeya." She then smiled, looking kind of ashamed, "I really don't know why I came. I guess just to talk, to show off this silly ability I have," she motioned to her lovely, petite female body before continuing. "And all in all, I just have no idea what to say." Suddenly tears welled up in her eyes, "My entire species was eradicated from the planet, my final lucid memory was being on fire and hoping I could save Tess, and now...now...."

Suddenly she was crying full force, sobbing. Deeya came over to her on the bed and wrapped her arms around the woman. "It will be okay, Silus, you are alive."

The woman laid her head against Deeya chest and continued crying while saying, "All my friends, my family...all gone...."

Deeya petted the woman's blonde hair and shoulders as she cradled the crying beauty. Deeya finally said, "I was orphaned before I was old enough to know my parents. While you were sleeping, my parents were on another continent and the sky fell onto the world. Nearly everyone died all around me. When the refugees assembled in the only city that had any buildings left in it, they soon realized, I was the only elven baby there, the only elf at all."

Silus wiped away tears, looking at the pain of the past in Deeya's face before pushing herself back up. Deeya settled back into her cross-legged position again. They sat close, knees touching, there was an intimacy between them, shared trauma in a way. Deeya felt slightly uncomfortable, but she also couldn't deny that her and Silus shared something by opening up.

Deeya could still smell the fragrance of the soap Silus had used to bathe. It made Deeya wonder if that was something Silus controlled with her/his shapeshifting ability. Silus wiped her eyes and said, "Tess has many memories of people telling her about the catastrophe. So much of that side of the world was devastated. Everyone thought that the entire side of the continent had sunk, and the seas were not fit for travel, especially since pretty much all the ships in the entire world were destroyed."

Deeya nodded, "The main point of the story is," Deeya paused to reach out and take Silus's hand in her own as she continued, "I kind of have an understanding of what it's like to be as alone as you feel. Sure, much later in life, I was able to return to my kind, but...none of them were like me. So, again, I found myself alone. I was born an elf, but raised by humans and dwarves. I am looked at with awe by humans and among the elves...I feel like they are some strange species of people I will never understand."

Silus squeezed Deeya's hand, "Our situations are different, yet the same." She cocked her head to the side, "I do not think I ever would have realized."

Deeya laughed. "Life has a funny way of working."

Silus laughed as well, a cute giggle that lit up the room. "That it does, Bard, that it does." She then reached up and pulled her bodice forward. The adjustment revealed more skin than Deeya had been ready for, a reminder that this was a borrowed form. She looked away as Silus reached within her top, while saying, "I do have something special for you, though." She smiled at Deeya, when she realized Deeya was looking away so as not to see down Silus's top. She then produced a piece of parchment. "Here." Deeya took the small, folded paper and started to unfold it while Silus tried to readjust her top over her breasts, "Ugh, how do you women live with these things, they never seem to sit right."

Deeya laughed and shook her head. As she opened the paper fully, she said, "Seems like I could ask you the same thing about a certain other part of your regular anatomy. Especially with the size yours is."

Silus finished adjusting her ample bosom and said, "Oh the cock? Yeah, I just shrink it. One of the benefits of being who I am."

Deeya looked over the paper before reading it and said, "You can control specific parts like that?"

As Deeya watched, Silus's bust started increasing, spilling out of her dress. For a moment, Deeya thought the dress was going to explode open, but then the expansion stopped and went back to normal. Deeya pressed her bottom lip into her top lip and then said, "Fascinating." After she said that, Silus's dress shifted. The neckline plunged nearly to her belly button, the taut fabric flattening her chest with deliberate tension. The effect was theatrical and calculated, and the resulting décolletage was impossible for Deeya not to notice.

The display was titillating, but it was also interesting, and Deeya couldn't tear her eyes away as Silus molded the body like clay, clothes and all. Just as Deeya could be impressed by what she was seeing, Silus changed everything back to Shanice in her servant's gown.

"The clothes are you as well?" Deeya asked incredulously.

"Yes," Silus confirmed with a smile. "With a thought, I could be completely naked." The smile grew into a licentious grin. "You want to see?"

Deeya frowned, not really giving the proposal any form of consideration, but her image formed in her mind before she could stop her mind from wandering there.

"Wait...," Deeya said, pushing the thought aside. "If you control the clothes, then you did not need to be naked after you escaped the column of water...."

Silus laughed. "Yeah, Tessa would not have allowed that. She insists on making things... convenient," she said with a twinkle in her eye.

Deeya put her face into her hands and breathed in and out exasperatedly as she rubbed her eyes. "I could have been spared seeing that, you know...."

Silus grinned largely and said, "Sorry, Deeya." He then changed his female face from Shanice's to Tessa's and said, "You know, I could change this all to Tessa and prance around for you some more, if you haven't gotten tired of her scrumptious body."

Deeya blushed and laughed, "I do not think I could tire of that body of hers, but I do admit that I have seen enough nudity for one stay here."

Silus turned her face from Tessa's back to Shanice's face. "I understand, but honestly, I don't think there could ever be enough female nudity for me," he said with a wink.

Deeya smirked and looked at the paper. It was a song, a ballad of sorts. It told the story of a vampire vagabond. His life was a busy time of killing innocents and raping, when he stumbled into an area with a dragon overlord. He eventually slew the dragon and became lord of the area. The humans lauded him as their hero and willingly became his subjects. "Is this the story of the first vampire king?"

"Yes," replied Silus. "It was a ballad that had been written about Tessa's grandfather, how he started the vampire empire. After the events in that story, he rallied all the vampires in the world to his stronghold, which became the capital of the new country, made peace with all nations, and brought a new era to the world. That peace lasted a few millennia. Tessa was the last vampire born to his line and had only made it through twenty years in life when the war came to the gates of the capital. I was several hundred years older." She then smiled and said, "I copied that song from memory. I'll be sure to make more before you come again. I was always a fan of bards, I listened to every song I could, even writing some of them down. I was never the greatest singer, but I tried."

Deeya grinned and grabbed Silus's hand, "Thank you for this. I look forward to more."

Silus put her other hand on Deeya's hand and said, "I'm glad you like it. Long lost songs from a long lost era. I was hoping they would be valuable to one such as yourself."

Deeya nodded and smiled gratefully. Silus then said, "We should go back to the suite, Tess should be about ready for breakfast."

Deeya nodded, stood, and put the paper away in her pack. When she stood, she caught Silus looking at her bottom. "Sorry," Silus said, not ashamed, just honest. "It's easy to see why you draw attention."

Deeya laughed and said, "Thank you for flattering me." It was a response she always had in store for those that actually seemed to respectfully admire her. Unlike the other type of admiring, which usually sounded like, "Damn, I want to rip those off of you," or "How much for one night?" Yeah, those could go to hell....

Silus shrugged her response to Deeya and then hugged her again when she got close. The hug lingered for a good time and Deeya allowed it to. It was a warm sincere hug, one that Silus needed to give. The woman was warm, she smelled good, she was soft, and gorgeous. For the first time, Deeya actually understood why Silus sought her out and came in the guise of a woman. Silus needed a friend, as simple as that. As she thought about the idea of her and the woman hugging her becoming friends it became harder to believe there was such a well-endowed man within her. Silus stepped back from the hug and smiled. "Let's go."

She took Deeya's hand, and they stepped out the door into the hallway. No one was around and Deeya locked the door behind them, though she decided not to do her paranoid door handle trick this time. Deeya followed Silus down to the second level and as they were about to enter the broom closet beside the stairs, a patron emerged from their room two doors down and spotted them. He was a merchant, high class, and looked to be making ready to leave for the day. He did not look as though his eyes were adjusted, as he blinked as if he was trying to understand what he was seeing, so it was doubtful he could tell anything about who he was looking at, outside of the fact that they were two girls and one of them belonged to the staff. Silus quickly grabbed Deeya in a suggestive way, wrapping an arm around her waist, and pulled her into the closet like she was about to enjoy a tryst. She even flashed a smile and a wink towards the merchant as she did it.

Both of them were shut in the broom closet, before Silus could open the secret back panel. It was a bit tight, as they squished their bodies together, Silus's throat pressed into Deeya's chest at one point and their lips were less than an inch away from each other's. It would have been a very compromising position to be caught in.

Silus struggled to reach around Deeya as she felt for the latch to the panel, as she did, Deeya felt all different muscle groups play against her. Finally, the panel flew open, and both women fell outwards into the secret passage. Deeya knew that the plan had been a good escape, but...the result of being so close to another woman was still shocking.

Silus stumbled with her, but they both caught themselves before hitting the floor. Silus giggled. "Shame you didn't fall, I could have fallen on top of you, and you would have gotten a face full of this cleavage," Silus said with a theatrical squeeze of her chest, flashing a grin Deeya had come to expect from the two licentious vampires.

Deeya smiled and shook her head. "Yeah, you and Tessa make a perfect pair."

Silus laughed and led the way. When they finally entered Tessa's suite, Tessa was standing in the same style dress as she normally wore. It reminded Deeya so much of a pirate look, and Deeya would know, considering a dark time in her past.... The leather pants, the loose laced up shirt; which was white this time; that showed far too much cleavage, and straps everywhere to hold all manner of things, including straps that seemed to just be worn as a corset. She looked at Silus and said, "My goodness, it has been so long since I have even thought of that face."

Silus smiled and said, "Sorry, I was just showing off for Deeya."

Tessa smiled and sauntered towards Silus, she took Silus's face in her hand and said, "That female vampire could kiss better than any female I had ever kissed, and her tongue could do things to my pussy that even I still don't understand." She smiled as the petite blonde woman turned into the male Silus; tall, splendid, and clothed in a very regal looking suit. Tessa then said, "But nothing has ever made me cum like this man's cock." She then looked at Deeya and said, "So what did you think of the woman who this guy used to fantasize over?"

Deeya laughed and said, "Oh, she was very pretty."

Tessa laughed, "That she was...and the things she could do with her mouth.... You might be a fool to resist me, Deeya, but you would have been a bigger fool to resist this woman's tongue...." She stroked Silus's cheek, looked at him with a smile and said, "Shame she never took your maleness into her mouth, I would have liked to have known how good she was at that sort of thing...."

Silus took Tessa's hand and kissed it. "No one has ever outdone you, my love."

Tessa looked into his eyes and for a moment, Deeya could see the love in her eyes, the fondness, and the pure joy of looking at him. But it was a fleeting moment. She then turned her smile to Deeya and said, "Sit, dear Bard, let us eat."

Breakfast had been laid out on the table in the suite. It was a feast of eggs, sausage, bread, cheese, and bacon. A breakfast that a king would be jealous of. As Deeya sat, she asked about the letter.

Tessa looked out of the window, down in the bar below. There was a man in a funny uniform talking to the barkeep. "That would be the delivery man now, verifying that this is where you are staying."

Deeya nodded while piling food onto her plate. Silus sat and did the same, saying, "It is truly amazing how you never realize you are missing something, until you are frozen into a pillar of water for a millennia."

Tessa cupped Silus's face, tilting it up to hers, and said, "Or have what you miss most frozen within a cage as clear as glass."

Silus smiled and rubbed his cheek into her palm. Deeya had to admit they were a cute, doting couple. It reminded her of her youth; of the first person she ever thought she loved. Before he became the man who taught her what love was not.

She shoved that distasteful thought aside and let her mind drift to Aloucia of the Fae and how the wild, wolf girl would nuzzle her and cuddle her. It almost hurt Deeya's heart to know they were still together, still had nights like that now and then, but Aloucia always left before the warmth could settle. She needed to be free, to roam, and Deeya had long since learned to let her. She sighed and ate her eggs, trying to forget about the past and wonder about the future, specifically the letter that was now making its way up to them.

The delivery boy had been exchanged from the barkeep to a serving maid and was now walking with

Deeya's letter along the catwalk. Deeya sipped the
orange fruit juice that was available, waiting, as Silus ate
and Tessa watched the bar below, sipping on a cup of
pungent dark liquid.

Finally, a knock came, and Tessa bid the barmaid
and the messenger to enter. The pair strode forward.
Deeya's focus was upon the letter in the man's hand, but
she could not help but notice how the barmaid had many
a sideways look at Silus. Deeya found it odd that Tessa
had not enlightened her staff on the new co-owner
situation. But then, maybe, they were trying to figure
out how to tell everyone that there was a new
shapeshifter on staff.…

The messenger bowed before Tessa and said,
"Mistress Tessa, I have a letter for one of your patrons, a
bard by the name of El'Mindeeya Do'Katal."

Tessa smiled and said, "That is the elf you seek,
sitting there."

The messenger stood up from the bow, then
kneeled before Deeya and said, "Ma'am, I have a letter for
you, can you prove who you are?"

Deeya pointed at the small emerald resting within
her clavicle. It dangled from the black choker
embroidered with wolves, which she always wore. "I am
the Emerald Bard, a daughter of Fo'Est, and this trinket
is part of the Emerald Stone, the largest emerald ever
found, which was given to me by a dear friend."

The man nodded and said, "That is one of the
passwords. Here is your letter." Deeya took the letter
from him with a smile.

Before she could tip him, Tessa handed the man several golden coins and said, "Thank you, dear sir. May your journey be safe."

The man bowed deeply and left the room, followed by the barmaid who shut the door behind them.

Deeya looked closely at the parchment in her hand. It was folded and sealed. The small wax seal bore the crest of House Kell, the rulers of a kingdom that Deeya had wanted to avoid due to the rumors she had heard about the political strife there. She broke the seal, unfolded the small document, and, due to the perfume on the parchment, she knew exactly who had wrote it before she even glimpsed upon the first word:

> How long has it been? How many words have been left unsaid? How many words have needed to be said? I wish I held the answers, my beautiful green bard, but alas, I do not. All I know is this: I need you, just as you needed me on our first adventure. Part of me doesn't expect you to come, after my last letter…. But part of me remembers who you are and waits with bated breath, impatiently, for you to arrive. You'll find my abode on the Avenue of White.
> --Ashengrey

She recognized the hand, she recognized the name, and, as mentioned before, she even recognized the smell that wafted up from the note itself. Ashengrey A'Taril was the blonde lover that Tessa had mentioned before. She was a Regal Elf, the higher born urban elves that loved society, even though she did not fit that mold in the slightest, as her past was the absolute most convoluted history Deeya had ever heard. She was a sorceress whose specialty was the manipulation of time. She was beautiful and Deeya loved her dearly, but they had also broken each other's hearts several decades earlier. And through all of this reading of the letter and reverie that followed, Deeya had not stopped to realize that she had completely stopped breathing.

Tessa was the first to realize something was odd, so she said, "Deeya, are you okay?"

Deeya's emerald eyes rose up to stare vacantly towards Tessa. Silus then realized that the bard was not breathing. He dropped his food, reached out his hand, grabbed Deeya's hand and said, "Bard, breathe."

With that, Deeya exhaled and quickly inhaled. Ashengrey showed Deeya that love could still happen, even after all Deeya had been through her own first love. The end of the relationship came when Ash had depended on Deeya to be somewhere, but Deeya had been on a quest she could not get away from. Apparently, Ash had almost died because of it. After the last letter she had received, before this one, from Ash, Deeya had promised never to love wholeheartedly again. Even though a few years later she met Aloucia and fell for her, she never fully invested herself to the wild wolf girl, which, secretly, was a regret that made her stoically resolved to be there for Aloucia in any way she could.

Everything inside Deeya changed in that moment, she could help Ash, and right the wrong she did to her. But then what? Get back with her? After the words that were exchanged? After decades of silence?

Deeya breathed slowly, tried to calm herself and force herself to come back to reality. Silus's voice said, "You look as if you were being strangled by a ghost."

Deeya put on a rueful expression and said, "I suppose I was."

Tessa frowned, "So who needs your help and how bad is it for you to react like that?"

Deeya looked up at her and said, "The blonde one."

Tessa nodded, "Ah, her. I remember her, you know." Tessa sat down in another chair at the table. "She was a beauty, but dangerous."

Deeya nodded and said, "That I know."

Tessa said, "What are you going to do?"

Deeya's eyes scanned the words again, she focused in on how Ash needed her like Deeya had needed Ash on their "first adventure together." She remembered it well. Deeya needed to find a long lost bardic artifact, had found reference to it being in an obscure cave. At the time, she and Ash were only just getting to know each other. Ash said that she needed something from the same area, so they went with each other. Deep inside the cave, they found…resistance. Deeya was not near the magical bard she was now, so without Ash's sorcery, she would not have come out of the cave alive, nor would she had found the artifact she sought.

Deeya smiled slightly, like it was a joke to herself, as she said, "Help her."

Tessa smirked and said, "You are too much of a helper."

Deeya shrugged and said, "It's what I do, kind of like my *Deal.*"

Tessa reacted instantly to Deeya's comment, but Silus was oblivious as he said, "Remember the warning from Tessa's vision."

Deeya shrugged again, stood, and said, "I have to right my wrong. I might have hurt her, she might have hurt me, but in the end, it all happened because of me starting this life I am on now."

Tessa then said, "I heard a story about you having to climb the floating mountains in Valley of the Wandering Earth. I also heard that this blonde girl, Ashtari, Ash-Trey, Ash-something?"

"Ashengrey"

"Yes, that's it. I heard she had been killed while you did so."

Deeya frowned, looking down at the seat she had just vacated, not able to meet anyone's eyes, "Almost. She was almost killed, and I wasn't there for her."

Silus then said again, "Do not make this decision lightly. It is one that will reverberate throughout your life."

Deeya grinned and kissed the stoic, beautiful man on the cheek. "Every decision that involves love does. Especially when it's the love that teaches you love isn't just a story."

She bid them both goodbye. She was leaving when the two smiled and squeezed each other's hand at her comment as she left. She did not stop by her room very long. Just long enough to make sure everything was stowed correctly before she threw her pack over her shoulders and left. Tessa watched the Emerald Bard walk out of the Darkened Deal from her vantage point in her suite. She put her hand on the glass and said, "Goodbye, Emerald Bard, and good luck."

Deeya turned her head to look up at the windows of Tessa's suite, as if she heard the words herself. She smiled, waved, and blew a kiss to the raven-haired vampress who owned the inn, before she turned, walked out the door and let it shut behind her.

2: A Symphony of Old Debts

Movement 1: Strangers

The table in the far corner was dark. Deeya had learned that there was always at least one such table in every form of watering hole. That deep, dark table where people did business not meant to be seen. Deeya had been to this dive of a tavern once before, though it had been decades and decades ago, during her dark years. No matter how many times seedy taverns changed over time, they always stayed the same.

Deeya stood her pack in the seat and sat beside it. She then picked up the glass of dark wine that was waiting there for her and sipped it, while leaning back into the seat, as she stared out at a stage she had never played upon. Across from her sat a bearded man, cloaked in shadows that Deeya dare not look at or acknowledge yet. Instead, she sat there, relaxed, sipping her dark wine and thinking about how much history repeats itself. The last time she was in this bar, she stood guard at the door while the leader of her adventurer group sat across from a bearded man cloaked in shadows. They had been hired to rob a caravan between here and the city of Norvale, which was the provincial seat of the province of Norvale. Norvale had been her destination, until she got the message that sidetracked her here....

"El'Mindeeya Do'Katal, the Emerald Bard. To what do I owe this honor?" The words were gruff yet silent, and obviously sarcastic.

"'Tis been far too many years for you to bring up honor...," Deeya replied, distaste dripping from her tone.

The man guffawed silently and leaned forward, his voice becoming a whisper, "What do you know about Cavan Quinlan?"

Deeya actually had discovered quite a bit of information through collecting rumors about him in her travels. Now that she had been drawn into his province, she was starting to consider herself an expert. She sipped her wine again, enjoying the berry flavors, buying herself some time to consider what exactly to admit to knowing. "He's the duke of this province and his castle is in the capital city of Norvale, which is just a league away."

"He beats his wife and daughter," the man said with a matter-of-fact tone.

Deeya didn't seem to care, "As do most human men."

"I see you still harbor a hatred. The king is asking for you to get rid of him."

Deeya scoffed loudly, too loudly for the man in the shadow's liking, "I'm a bard, not an assassin."

"You are a woman indebted to King Kell and you were told never to come back here."

Deeya finished her drink and sighed, "I am here to help a friend."

"You will find your friend in Duke Quinlan's dungeon, not in her home. You will find what the King is now demanding of you might be beneficial to yourself." Deeya's finally turned her eyes to the man in the shadows. Her glare held back none of the poison she felt for this man at all, she hated being a pawn, but her and the Kell dynasty had a history, once that she obviously could not ignore. The man continued as the elven female stood and picked up her pack, "You will find Ashengrey greatly changed."

Deeya hesitated, hating that the mention of Ash's name garnered a reaction. She collected herself quickly though and replied, "I have no doubt, as when her and I last spoke, I was assured it was for the last time.... Good day, Prince Kell."

The man said nothing as he watched the lithe, elven woman stride away, while his blue eyes twinkled in the dim candle light that only hit them when he leaned forward. She had a night ahead of her, a long trek that would lead her into a pit of vipers he doubted even she could be prepared for. Her journey would not only test all her loyalties, but test the loyalties of her own heart....

--

Deeya had never minded traveling at night. Her elven night vision had always served her well. She looked up at the night sky. The Wolf Moon hung as a sliver against the vast array of twinkling stars. It had been two weeks since the events at the

Darkened Deal and she was still unsettled by what had transpired.

The cool night air helped her think as she walked along the road. An old bard's song came to mind about traveling in the dead of night. It spoke about passing through towns and villages when no one saw you pass through. It asked the question, if no one saw you, were you really even there? The idea made the midnight traveler seem more of a ghost than anything else. Since Deeya could easily see all the other travelers on the road, when they could not see her, she was easily able to avoid them, passing through the night unseen.

And she *was* a ghost on this night. She walked in the shadows of the night, avoiding the random camp fires, and other signs of life. Humans that were too ignorant to seek a fire or too poor for an inn were all too easy to avoid, especially with their limited vision. Since the only moon in the sky was just a sliver, the night was so dark it was a wonder that those with limited non-elven vision did not stumble in a hole on the road.

Deeya trekked on and in the early morning hours, the elf clad in dark green attire strode through the city gates. She wore a simple travel pack, which had her lute strapped to the left side of it, in a slip case to keep it from the elements. Her green jacket over her dark green vest kept her warm against the cool morning chill, though being an elf she really had no need of it. The vest was just low cut enough to prove she was a woman, but still in her modest style, and her green leather pants were very form fitting, and tucked into her green leather boots. When Deeya walked through any town, there was never any guess as to her being the Emerald Bard, and this city was no exception.

The streets were mostly deserted at this hour, as shops were busy loading carts and vendors were still setting up in the market center. Deeya strode on through without giving much of anything her attention besides her thoughts.

Ash...why have you contacted me....

She remembered the note well, a note with no address, no city name, only a small clue. The Avenue of White. Norvale was not considered a notable city upon the face of the planet, yet it was known for one thing. Just outside the city were stone quarries that mined the whitest building stone ever discovered. The flawless white stone was used all over the world, although the city it came from was generally not discussed, as the businessmen here sold to tradesmen who sold the stone elsewhere, making a fortune. The business model was flawed beyond belief, as the city here was poor. All, except those that lived on this particular street....

The Avenue of White was an avenue filled with rather large mansions made out of the expensive stone. There were only two types of people that lived on this street. Regal Elves who wanted their money to buy status that their elven blood demanded, and the tradesmen that made the most off of the stone by peddling it as their own brand to cities at the far reaches of the continent, and sometimes beyond. The street was less than half a mile long, lined with solid white, multistory mansions, all looking as similar as anyone could possibly imagine a street full of solid white buildings could possibly be.

As expected, though, she found the correct house easily. The building was the same as many of the others on the street. Completely nondescript, except for two very small details. This house, unlike any of the others that looked exactly the same, had potted plants on the steps. That alone proved to Deeya that it belonged to Ashengrey A'Taril. When last Deeya saw her, she was every inch a Regal Elf, outwardly. There were many differences between Forest and Regal elves, but the most obvious were that Regal Elves were tall and blonde, that and the fact that Regal Elves hated nature.

Deeya's early life, long before she became a traveling bard, was full of hardship and abuse. She rose out of that, vowing to never love again, never get involved again. But Ash changed all that, Ash was Deeya's first true love, as Ash was the first to ever truly love the bard back. But above it all, Ash was the first person Deeya had ever hurt emotionally. And even though Deeya had been beaten by her first lover, she was more devastated by what had transpired between them.

She slowly climbed the steps to the house, noticing how the potted plants needed some attention. As she walked by them, she hummed lightly, and the plants seemed to perk up a little, maybe even seem to be greener after she passed. The door was as ornate as the expensive stone building material of the building would suggest. The carvings seemed to tell a story about the building of the house. But there, right in the middle of the door, was the second sign Deeya needed to see to prove that it was Ashengrey's house. Although, seeing such an embellishment, not only stopped the bard in her tracks, it made her breath catch a little bit.

The knocker was a lute. Deeya tried not to let her heart race at the thought of an embellishment meant to represent her. It was probably just the embellishment to point out to Deeya that she was at the right house.

Yeah, that's exactly what it is.... It had to be, right?

She stood there in front of the door, her heart pounding, not from fear, but memory. She took a breath and steadied herself as she mentally ran through the instructions that came hidden inside the letter she had received in the Darkened Deal. With a glance around the street, she reached under the balustrade next to the stairs and retrieved the key. Without hesitating, without letting her nerves fail her, she put the key in the lock, turned it, and entered the home of her former and most intense love.

As the door closed behind her, she reached back to her backpack with her left hand and retrieved the sword that was sheathed between her back and her pack. At the same time she retrieved the axe hanging off her left hip. In her left hand she had an elven short sword, wide and sharp, great for attacking and blocking, the other was a small axe, akin to a tomahawk, but it seemed to resonate with some sort of energy, like it sensed her worry about danger, but she kept the axe silent. The axe head was not normal either, as it was shaped in the form of a treble clef and bass clef merged together into a single symbol.

The room before her was completely destroyed.

Deeya instantly recognized the scene, the whole house had been rifled through as if someone had been searching for something. Her melancholy had vanished as she turned on her investigator mode and she slowly went through the house, lifting things with sword tip and axe blade, touching nothing, taking note of everything in her mind. The entire house had been ransacked, even the hidden room that Deeya knew Ash would have. In the bedroom was where Deeya found the only thing that had been originally out of place in Ash's house.

As previously mentioned, Regal Elves almost inevitably shunned nature, especially Ash. Nature was chaotic, where architecture always had smooth lines and useful functionality. The tree in the corner opposed this. Deeya approached the potted tree, which was strong, even though it obviously did not have the best caretaker. The soil in the pot had been dug through, but not overly much. Deeya sheathed her sword, and reached between the branches, felt around the leaves, and found the note.

This is all playing out too weirdly, thought Deeya. The detective side of her was getting paranoid. It had every right to get that way. She was being led as if she were on a leash. A pawn. She then sighed and opened the note and read the hidden message:

> Hello my beautiful green bard. If you are reading this, then I have been imprisoned. You will soon find the conspiracy that put me there. Few know you as I do, few know you can solve this riddle. I am truly sorry to involve you, sorry to pick at old wounds, but I need you. I promise, when this is over, we shall say the words that need to be said.
> --Ashengrey

Deeya crumpled the letter and burnt it in the smoldering coals of the fireplace that she had stoked earlier to see if they were still warm. They had not been, but her stoking them with a song warmed them, which warmed the room. She knew, beyond a shadow of any doubt, that she had just walked into a hornet's nest. Ash was imprisoned, an abusive Duke had a firm grip over the city, along with his sorceress lover, and above it all there was a mystery that people were trying to get her to solve. The prince obviously did not want the Duke removed, he wanted her to not see what else was going on.

There was only one place to start, she decided. She left the house through a back door, and blended in with the morning traffic which was in full swing in the road. The way to the jail was easy to find, though the conversation she was going to have, she knew, was going to be anything but....

--

The hustle and bustle of the streets were in full swing. The markets were open with all their stands stocked. Deeya partially regretted not storing her lute somewhere, as the likelihood of her being recognized as *The* Emerald Bard went up quite a bit. Through the cacophony of sound, though, she never actually heard any form of overt recognition. Some whispered that she must be *a* bard, but nothing further than that. It had been decades since she had visited this region, so the likelihood of being recognized was hopefully quite low.

The jail itself was located towards the center of the city. It was part of what was known as the "Old Inner Keep of Norvale." There were three standing "castles" within the city, two of which were located inside a courtyard surrounded by an ancient stone wall. The third was actually part of that wall. The two on the inside were large, towering structures that dominated the city. The other, though, was smaller, more of a stone building. The smaller structure had three purposes. The armory and guard's barracks existed on the top floor, the only floor above ground, but below the structure was a latticework of underground facilities where prisoners were kept.

Together, all three "castles" looked imposing, even though the smaller of the two larger buildings was falling into ruin. Oddly, though, the disrepair of the building added to the gothic charm of the city of Norvale. Many inns in the area, as well as businesses, catered to the old world feel in architectural design and artwork.

She entered the courtyard and looked up at the ancient stone structures, marveling at what humans accomplished so very long ago. Sure, there were many larger, more intricate structures in the world, but this one had stood the test of time far longer than some entire countries. She then turned her eyes to the training guards, as their shouts and grunts echoed off the stone buildings and walls around the courtyard. Humans could do amazing things, if only they would get their heads out of their asses and stop warring....

The guardsmen trained with all manner of weapons and fighting styles. Norvale was not a place that regularly saw wars, being almost dead center of the country, but the guards of the city needed to be ready for anything, as crime was a never ending problem. As with most civilized cities in the world the city guards kept the peace under a magistrate of some kind. Normally, the judicial system consisted of a judge, or judges, and sometimes a jury. Lawyers, bounty hunters, and private detectives were the people's only defense against a tyrannical judicial system. This city, as with most cities, revolved around land trading and money.

Deeya always hated prisons and jails. She had been in a few but had never been officially charged with anything that would ever stick. Normally it was silly charges, the typical bard stuff, inciting riots, being at the wrong place at the wrong time, or some drunk attacked her and she made sure he never attacked anyone ever again.

As she stood outside the building, she thought very hard about going in without being seen. After a long sigh, she knew that it was not the way to do things. Once she was inside, the assistant magistrate took her pack which had her lute strapped to it, her sword, her axe, and all the easily found other weapons she had strapped to her in some fashion, which mainly consisted of a handful of throwing knives. After she had finished with unarming, she took one final look at her pack, as she hated leaving it anywhere so public, before she entered the prison itself.

The prison was decent, as decent as prisons could be, really. The prisoners appeared well fed and were in good spirits. Ash's cell was in the far back, where they kept the truly dangerous prisoners. The fact of the matter was that she was a sorceress, and magic users were rare in the world, and dangerous. They were almost uncontainable.

The cell itself was a dual cell system. A "larger" room was the main cell and inside it stood several very small cells around the walls. The cells had just enough room to lay down in, if you did not roll over. There were no beds. Each cell had a chamber pot and chains. The chains were on a pulley system. When no one was in the room to be enchanted, the chains were loosened and the prisoners could move around. When someone was to come into the room though....

"Prisoner, stand and prepare for your restraint."

The guard's voice was rough and commanding. There was a sound of chains rustling. When the sound stopped the guard reached over a chair to pull the lever beside the door. The sounds of chains rustling happened again, yet far more rattled. The sound resonated throughout the jail as a large system of counterweights and pulleys pulled all the chains in all the cells taut. When the sound ended, the guard removed her keys and unlocked the door. She then opened the door and pointed towards a cell in the darkest corner of the small room. There were three cells against the three walls of the room that did not contain the entrance door. There, in the far corner to the right of the door was a woman. She was the only prisoner in the room, but the guard still said, "That's her, over there." As Deeya entered, the gruff looking woman said, "I'll stay here in this chair to release her restraints when you are done with her."

The cell door shut and locked it behind her. Deeya looked across the room at the woman chained tightly to the wall behind the bars. It was hard to recognize the blindfolded elf chained to the wall, at first. The woman was blonde and taller than Deeya. Her tattered clothes hung unevenly, grime obscuring much of her skin. Behind the filth, Deeya could make out cuts and bruises, some of the caked on dirt was probably blood. With her arms stretched above her, Deeya could make out the strain in her muscles, the subtle signs of someone who hadn't let captivity weaken her completely.

They feared this woman and they knew how her magic worked. The blindfold was a strip of leather that tightly covered her eyes, wrapped around her ears and below the base of her skull. It was shackled at the back, impossible to take off. Very few people could control magic in the world and those that did, either hid their powers, or lived by them. Magic worked in many different ways, most assault spells worked on visual cues, as in the target had to be seen. Sometimes even the magic itself had to be seen to be cast.

Ashengrey A'Taril had controlled and had mastered a form of magic that could control minds, confuse people, and make people see something that was not there, or even not see something that was there in front of them. But what truly made her dangerous was a secret only a handful knew of, was Ash could control time. The blindfold kept her from casting a good deal of her magic. She was a danger to their society, or at least she was a danger to those who thought she was a danger to them.

Her ragged clothes might be torn and dirtied, but mostly they showed the marks of neglect and cruelty. Deeya wondered if she had been whipped on her back, but she pretty much doubted that concept, as that would mean she would have to be taken off the wall. Looking at the visible signs, though, Deeya concluded that Ash was not permanently damaged.

Deeya slowly approached the chained woman, remembering all the things she had tried not to hear the guardswoman saying. Deeya tuned her out the instant the woman said that no elf was to be trusted, unless behind bars, as if Deeya, herself, was not obviously an elf. As the blond woman heard the footsteps approaching, she raised her head, almost as if she could see Deeya. In a tired voice, a voice that sent a shockwave through Deeya, she said, "A visitor?"

The guard might have been on the other side of the door, several feet away, but Deeya took no chances. She started to hum a tune. It was a quick tune to a piece of magic that would make it impossible for people outside of a few meters to eavesdrop. The voice, in a less tired, inquisitive way said, "Bard?"

The spell was set and Deeya said, "The one you requested."

Against all odds, the blond before Deeya almost smiled. "Hello, Deeya. They actually let you in?"

"I once told you a bard can go anywhere and do anything, it's why I'm so good at being me."

Ash actually smiled then, only to have her smile go away as she lowered her head. She said the first thing she absolutely had to say to the woman before her, "I'm sorry."

Deeya's response was instant and bitter, "Do not ever apologize to me, after what I did.... There is no forgiveness for me, so never ask for forgiveness for anything you ask of me, or get me into." As much as

Deeya still loved Ash, there was still what had happened. It had been decades since they last spoke, decades since their two hearts shattered, decades since deeds and words were done and said that could not be undone or unsaid.

"Deeya...." Ash's voice trailed off as she could not find the words to say anything to continue the line of how sorry she truly was. She knew Deeya would never forgive her nor would the bard ever forgive herself, so Ash decided to completely drop the issue and focus on the task at hand. When Deeya was in work mode, she was nothing if not single minded. "What have you learned so far?"

"Nothing besides you still looking amazing, even if you are...here."

Ash blushed. Despite everything, Deeya's words could pull a smile from her and warm her blood. She had no way of knowing the crash course in flirting that Deeya had just gone through and survived. Ash knew that Deeya was a charmer, she always had been. A poet who could melt the hardest man or melt a prisoner being held in a dungeon who had given in to her fate.... "Deeya, the Duke found out that I have ties to his "mother.""

"Nice to see bigotry is still alive and well," Deeya's words dripped with poison. "But I also know the woman posing at his mother is not his mother, I hear she's an elf."

"Correct. The official reason I am in here is because I'm an elven sorceress, but I think there is far more going on.... I fear...." She could hear Deeya lean against the bars, the smell of the bard reached her nostrils. The scent carried traces of the forest air and old songs winding through the trees. Deeya's smell was wild, familiar, and painfully grounding. "I fear my sister is behind all of the crazy things going on."

And just like that, Deeya was no longer near the bars. "I thought she was dead."

"As did I.... Deeya be careful, she's more powerful than me."

This entire subject turned into an old wound that tugged at the very reason they turned their back on each other's love. "I hate time travel...," Deeya said spitefully.

"As do I, that's why I don't do it...."

Deeya finished the sentence for her, "Unless you *have* to." After a moment's hesitation, as Deeya watched Ash's head follow her movements, she said, "So the Duke is her son?"

"No. That is the real reason I am in here. Deeya, I was here trying to find her, to finish her, to find out how she survived our encounter."

"The encounter you wrote about?"

Deeya obviously meant the letter Ash had written that tore Deeya's heart from her chest. The one in which Ash lamented about how she had finally achieved victory, but it cost her and she almost died because a certain emerald wearing bard could not be trusted to show up at a particular place at a particular time.

"Yes, that encounter. Deeya, I've tracked her across time, I still do not know how she did it. I tracked her here, yet I had no clue she had embedded herself with the Duke."

Deeya was close to the bars again, Ash could smell her, which made it hard for her to concentrate on what Deeya said, "So she's controlling the duke personally?"

Ash looked directly at where she believed Deeya's face was, picturing it in her mind. She had feared this day, when she went back in time and faced the Deeya that was still going through all of this mess. "The duke has imprisoned his wife. My sister is impersonating his mother, but they are actually lovers. He apparently denies that she is even an elf, and she hides her ears because of it."

Deeya sighed heavily, "Alright, I'll get to work...."

Ash pictured the bard leaving in her mind's eye and said, "Be careful, my beautiful, green bard."

"Always, my love."

Deeya strode away, canceling her magic spell and left Ash in silence. Soon, Ash knew, they would bring her food. She wondered why they had not beat her more than just this slight superficial roughing up they had given her. She knew the psychological stuff was worse, but still, humans were a crude bunch and capable of more. In the silent darkness of the cell, after her chains were released, she sat cross-legged and re-entered the meditation that Deeya would eventually get around to teaching her.

She quickly discovered, though, that she could not reach her center, she could still smell Deeya. Freshly fallen leaves and growing things... a scent she had never forgotten. Time travel was a funky business, as she knew that Deeya would prevail and eventually, they would become close again, but for now, the present was upon them both, and even giving the bard a hint of her future could change everything. Deeya had to be who she was right now to accomplish what she had to do right now.

Ash adjusted her tactic trying to enter meditation. She focused on the here and now, instead what would be in the future. This task would change Deeya to her core, test the truths she held about herself, and for the first time, Deeya was going to step out of her comfort zone and save the world...that is...if she could separate her

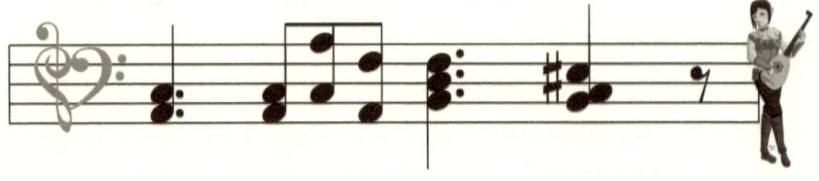

Movement 2: The Things We Do for Love

The party was nothing less than amazing. People twirled and danced in a waltz fueled by an orchestra, being conducted by an elven female wearing green. Her short-cropped hair contrasted the elegant outfit, but it suited her, framing her face with a sharpness that made her look every inch the conductor. She rarely dressed up in this way, but she always drug out the dressy attire for the bigger performances. It seemed to be less rare these days, since it had barely been a full three weeks since she had worn it last, at that country inn at the crossroads.

The outfit was most definitely not simple. It consisted of a top which wrapped around her chest which supported her breasts, which left her mid-section bare, except for fabric hanging down from the sides. The bottom was a half skirt with a front 'flap,' as she enjoyed calling it sarcastically, which hung down the front. The outfit was beautifully ornate, and unmistakably elven. Deeya rarely felt anything other than 'boyish,' but in this, she caught glimpses of something softer in herself, something she didn't often admit was there. It had golden embellishments all over, looking very much like tree branches, except for the obvious musical symbols, the most ornate of which was the Treble and Bass Clefs fused together into one symbol. Her footwear was the strappy elven shoes that almost left her feet bare as straps wove around her calves to just below her knee. Around her neck was the only piece of jewelry she never went anywhere without, the teardrop emerald dangling into her clavicle from the black, laced choker which was embroidered with wolves, and her dark green metallic vambraces which covered most of both of her forearms, but looked ornate enough to be part of the outfit.

To get to play this gig, Deeya had to 'work the crowd' as the term went. She started playing venues in town, and soon the Duke got word that the world-famous Emerald Bard was in town, and invited her to conduct the orchestra at this very ball at the end of the week. It had been a long few days, as Deeya's mind kept drifting back to Ash in the dungeons. She knew she could not go back, sooner or later, no matter her precautions, someone would see her coming and going, and there were only so much her mind wiping song, that made people forget recent events around them, could be useful.

She ended the waltz with the same flourish as the people dancing. As the music died, and she lowered her baton, the audience clapped in appreciation of the fun they had dancing, as well as the music itself. Deeya allowed herself to turn towards the audience and received the applause with a slight bow. The intermission was finally upon her. Before she could exit the stage, though, trumpets blared throughout the room. The room went quiet as the page by the door announced loudly, "The Duke's Mother! Ryn'Vey Con'Taril'Kal."

Deeya knew her moment had finally come, her first introduction to Ryn'Vey, Ashengrey's sister. Deeya took note of everything about the moment. The first thing she noted was the use of "Taril," which was her true family name, as it was also part of Ashengrey's family name. Secondly, it was obviously an elven name, the way in which it was broken up. From all the intelligence Deeya had gathered from the week she had spent within the city, trying to get this gig, it was obvious that the duke himself was a hardcore racist when it came to elves. There was plenty of propaganda around to support it, yet his mother using an elven name...sure not everyone inside this bustling, thriving city was stupid enough to not catch on to this obvious scandal.... Deeya was almost holding her breath to actually see Ryn'Vey herself, so she could see how elven the woman looked.

And then it happened, for in she walked. Deeya went from almost holding her breath, to almost choking. Ryn'Vey Con'Taril'Kal, the Duke's mother, was an exact copy of Ashengrey herself. She looked exactly like Ash, a perfect twin, yet instead of being dirty and bound to a wall, this woman was the air of regality and feminine beauty, and she was on display. Her blonde hair flowed down to her waist, far longer than Deeya had ever seen Ashengrey's. Her dress, a gorgeous white flowing gown with gold embellishments, emphasized every aspect of her feminine body, was unlike anything she could see

Ashengrey ever wearing. She seemed sculpted in a way that exaggerated her form, elegant and severe all at once, with a dress that seemed tailored to command attention.

The hair, once Deeya was able to concentrate again, stood out to Deeya very quickly, as it completely hid her ears. She had other elven features, but honestly, the societal elves and humans were very much alike in many aspects. They were the same height, and the blonde elven hair was only a shade lighter than most blonde humans. There was a build difference, but it was not unheard of for a human woman to be thin and athletic while being graceful and aloof.

For some unknown reason, at the sight of the twin to Ash, Deeya spontaneously realized that Ash had been vague about knowing if Ryn'Vey was here or not. Deeya had discovered, in the week since she had spoken to Ash, that Ryn'Vey was indeed here and indeed behind so many crazy goings on that she found herself not understanding how Ash could not know positively if she was here or not. And there she was, the elf that Ash called her sister, walking to her son and putting her arm on his shoulder.

The rumors she had learned within the week she had been in Norvale were the truly interesting aspect of what was going on with the Duke. One of the complete bonuses to being a bard was because people talk to and around them, not to mention how easy it was for bards to get into places where conversations happen. Deeya was the ultimate spy, because, seriously, who honestly pays attention to the entertainment.... It was during that time that Deeya started understanding far more of the picture that she could have ever guessed at. The Duke was using his 'mother' to make a power play for the throne that was owned by the Kell dynasty. It was destined to failure, unless he had some severe help. Deeya was able to fill in the obvious blank to the statement, though, as who better than a sorceress that could bend the wills of men, destroy a castle with a wave of the hand, and control time?

Even before Ash had told her, she doubted that the two were actually related. In fact, from what she could tell, the duke had been a great man until his mother showed up. Now, as Deeya's eyes fell upon the two together, seeing that there was no resemblance at all, Deeya knew that Ryn'Vey's sorcery was at work. Ash was powerful in the art of twisting the mind, though she never used it unless she had to. It was becoming painfully obvious that Ryn'Vey was in complete control of the Duke.

Deeya stepped down from the stage, entering the crowd and moved towards the throne, where the duke sat with Ryn'Vey at his shoulder. The guards let her approach and Ryn'Vey stepped around the duke to great her, saying, "You have an amazing talent. I take it you are an elf from the Forested Isle?"

"Thank you, milady. That I am, milady," replied Deeya obsequiously as she curtsied.

"I've only heard of you through reputation, I'm glad I could finally hear you." Deeya could not tell if the woman was lying, but she suspected it, even though she had no real reason to, as she doubted that Ryn'Vey knew about Deeya and Ash's prior relationship. Deeya was obviously just being paranoid, she hoped.... There was nothing more dangerous than standing in the lion's den, with the lion smiling beside, pretending not to bare its teeth at it looks over your exposed flesh and unarmored frame.

"I'm glad I have lived up to expectations."

Deeya allowed the woman to present her to the Duke. "Your Grace, I present tonight's entertainment, El'Mindeeya Do'Katal, the Emerald Bard."

"I did not expect you to be an Elf...," droned the Duke. Deeya quickly wondered if the duke's racism was part of Ryn'Vey's cover, which would be odd as she had no real cover to speak of, or if she kept the duke's original racism to not raise suspicion.

"The honor is all mine, your Grace," responded Deeya in a gracious tone.

Ryn'Vey bowed deeply with Deeya and then, together, the two females moved away, as Deeya's break was coming to an end. Then it happened, just as Deeya had been expecting, "Would you please join me for dinner tomorrow?"

Deeya felt the trickle of magic flow into her. She had taken precautions for something like this and responded as she knew she should have, "But of course, I would be delighted to join you for dinner."

Ryn'Vey smiled as the bard looked from her eyes to her chest, her eyes displaying a touch of lust. Ryn'Vey made sure Deeya got a good view of her cleavage before she touched Deeya's face with her hand, redirecting the bard's eyes back to her own, and said, "Good, I cannot wait to pick your brain. You've traveled the world, I long to hear of your exploits."

Deeya forced herself to lean into the touch, mimicking what she believed the spell wanted from her.

"I'm sure my stories will pleasure you," she practically purred as her stomach churned.

The woman smiled and said, "It looks as if your intermission is coming to an end."

Deeya blinked, as if in a dream like state, and said, "A shame, I was hoping to talk more."

The woman then looked deep into Deeya's eyes, a look that Ash had given her a number of times. Thankfully the woman did not have her sister's smell, but she was near identical. The trickle of magic flow into her again, Ryn'Vey was making damn sure that Deeya was going to come to this dinner on the morrow. "Tomorrow then."

A sigh caught in her throat, the word leaving her like a dream. "Tomorrow...."

It wasn't a long walk back to the stage, but Deeya made it look harder than it was. She needed Ryn'Vey to believe the spell had worked, every stumble a calculated note. When she mounted the stage again, she even tried to act as if she was coming out of a dream, going so far as shaking her head as if to clear it, before making sure all the orchestra was present and looking at her. She made the signal for the members of the orchestra to pick up their instruments and quickly check their tuning. Then, after a few seconds, she raised her baton and started the next song.

Deeya could not help but smile. The trap had been set, from both sides. Deeya never liked walking into a trap, but she had to, for the trap was a setup for her own trap. Ash feared this woman, and Ash was the most powerful, not to mention the most beautiful, woman she had ever known. Ash had murdered this woman, yet she

still lived, Deeya owed it to Ash to stop this woman.
Deeya owed it to the kingdom to stop a future coup.
Ryn'Vey was on the verge of making a mistake many
people had made in their lives; she was underestimating
a bard....

Later in the evening, when the music was over and
all the schmoozing she could stomach had been finalized,
Deeya left the venue. Deeya had been offered a room at
the castle, which she ever so politely declined. She told
the Duke's attendant that a long-time friend and barkeep
in the city owned a quant inn very close to the palace and
had been pleased to see the green clad elven bard.
Therefore, Deeya had felt more inclined to stay there, old
friends always trump posh invitations, right? The duke
was all too happy to not have a "dirty elf" under his roof.
The entire situation seemed to sit wrong with Deeya,
though, as she left, as it was getting preposterous to
Deeya that no one else seemed to notice that his mother
was indeed an elf, herself.

Deeya did take an offered carriage ride back to her
inn. It felt odd, to her, walking through the inn's
common room in her elegant performance gown. The
innkeeper, whom she had never met before she booked
the room in his inn earlier in the week, nodded to her as
she passed. When she got to the door to her room, she
held out her hand, close to, but not touching the door
handle. As she suspected, when she hummed, it turned a
soft red to her eyes. Someone had been in her room, as
they had every night she cared to stop by and check it.

Inside the room, nothing looked touched. Her
travel clothes were in a bundle on the end of the bed she
had never slept in. After checking all the nooks and

crannies in the room, looking for hidden persons or magic, she shut the curtains on the window, stripped, and donned those travel clothes; her casual, normally worn attire. The loose shirt was held snuggly by her corset and her pants fit like gloves. She missed her sword, but it was with her backpack and lute, hidden away at the one place she knew they would never look, which was also the place she was going to go to rest, as she had every other night of the week she had been in town.

No matter how much those that were in power seemed to be on to her, no one had tied to Ashengrey, which seemed odd. How could she be connected to this entire fiasco without anyone connecting her to it through Ash? The bard sat on the bed and pondered the conundrum for the millionth time while she waited. After a few minutes, she arose and snuffed the lights. In the dark she rebundled her performing garments and then sat down again. The waiting was always the hardest part of doing any form of sneaky anything. Finally, after she had given up trying to solve the puzzle before her, she slid open the window and slipped out into the night.

The cool air was brisk upon the roofs of the buildings as she traversed the city from above. She was not surprised to see sentries stationed in look out areas, but most of them were watching the streets, not the rooves. The Avenue of White seemed to shine brighter at night than any other street in the city, since the lanterns on the street were surrounded by polished white stone. Deeya was careful to slip into a back, upstairs window, which was Ashengrey's bedroom.

The house was still shockingly empty of habitation of any kind, and had to be kept dark. The first night Deeya stayed in the room she made the mistake of laying on Ash's bed. She was shocked to realize that she had forgotten Ashengrey's smell. It was a scent that smelled of a field in spring, the musky aroma of a woman who was not afraid of work, and the faint smell of burnt cinders, almost like brimstone. The instant the smell in those sheets hit her nose, Deeya was thrown back in her mind....

Ashengrey, her blonde hair flowing in the wind as she ignited the air within her hand and threw the flame at those trying to kill her and Deeya. Ashengrey, who took an arrow to the shoulder to save Deeya's life in a fight they could not win, until Deeya became passionately angry and discovered far more of her abilities than she knew existed. Ashengrey, who could not swim, which Deeya found out about as the pair were plummeting towards the ocean after narrowly escaping a mob of angry creatures who wanted to boil the two alive. Ashengrey, whose wet clothes had to be removed so they could dry, who kissed Deeya so tenderly that night that both women found a solace that neither knew existed, within each other's arms.

The memories of all the time spent with the blond elven beauty rushed over her like a wave, as did the climax she had brought herself to. Deeya hated herself after the euphoria had run its course. Mad at herself for loving Ashengrey despite everything. Mad at herself for doing something as impetuous as what she had done then and there. Mad at herself for not being there decades ago when Ash needed her.

On this night, though, after the performance, she removed her pack from its hiding place, stowed her gear, put it back where she got it from, and sat cross-legged on a chair across the room from the bed. Deeya slowed her breathing and quickly entered a meditative trance. Tomorrow, she had many things to do, but mostly, she had to put an end to Ryn'Vey….

--

Before the sun arose, Deeya was back out on the street. She hated leaving behind the sword, but she was happy to have her axe, among several other gadgets and weapons on her person. She had several stops before she walked into the obvious trap where she was to snap her own shut. The first step of anything that requires any subterfuge in the slightest, was to make sure she was acting perfectly natural….

She spent the day visiting taverns in the eastern part of the city looking for paying work for a musician. She knew she was not going to be playing that night, but on the next day brought promising opportunities: three taverns were seeking a bard for their stage, a local council member needed music lessons for a family member, and a cute young couple wanted Deeya to audition for a wedding scheduled later in the month.

Noon came and went, and as the sun finally approached the horizon, Deeya was escorted into the dining room of the castle. The dining room itself, was bright, with far too many shadows being cast about with all the different candles and torches. The castle was quiet, at least far quieter than it had been while Deeya had been conducting the orchestra the night before. Everything seemed far more deadly this evening, like everything around was part of some elaborate trap....

Deeya enjoyed wearing her casual attire to the castle, instead of her regal gown. She took pride in looking every inch the tomboy that she knew she was. Her mind wandered as she climbed the raised area beside the dining room. The area ran the length of the dining room and was for more important guests than those that ate at the regular table. The raised area was carpeted, had more expensive (and easier to move) furniture that could be moved around at will. A network of curtains, all of which were gathered up towards the ceiling, could be lowered and used to partition the area into makeshift rooms.

Today, it was more or less open, even the curtain that divided the dining rooms were divided. Deeya surmised that sometimes the Duke would eat upon the raised area with his court below him. To one side sat a small, ornate table that had been set for two. The chairs were ornate as well, though the designs looked more like a confusing mess to Deeya, as they followed no nature lines or logic.

For the moment, she allowed her mind to continue to wander, as she looked over the scene. This was probably where the trap would be sprung. But how it would come down, she could not fathom. She thought about all the ways it could happen. Ryn'Vey could try to seduce her, especially since she looked so much like Ash, she could try to poison her, or mind control her. So many ways for it to go meant so many things that could go wrong. Most of all, though, Deeya's mind wondered what Ryn'Vey would wear, as the woman dressed so differently from Ash, it made it easy to tell them apart.

Deeya took a seat at the small table. Sitting at the table reminded her of sitting upon the stage at a theatre. Finally, the curtains shifted at the end of the room and Ryn'Vey entered the dining room. She wore a form fitting red dress that wrapped around her neck like a collar, yet divided down her chest, inviting attention to exposed cleavage, the fabric drawn tight in sculpted curves. It exposed her shoulders, arms, and back. With every stride, her legs appeared from divides in the fabric of the skirt only to vanish again as the other leg appeared. Her shoes were the kind of shoes ladies wore to give themselves more height, yet Deeya could never wear because she could not balance on a single spike on the heel.

She wore little in the way of jewelry, except for a gaudy necklace that completely distracted from, instead of accentuating her cleavage. All in all, it was a stunning dress. If Ash had worn it, Deeya would have been salivating. Oddly, what killed it was the smile that the woman wore. It was wrong...all wrong indeed. Ash had particular smiles for particular occasions. The smile upon Ryn'Vey's lips was not any smile Deeya had seen Ash ever use. It only brought home the knowledge that the stunning blonde beauty walking towards Deeya was not Ash.

After the shock of imagining Ash inside that dress, came the shock that the elven female wore her hair up in an elaborate hairdo, which completely exposed her elven ears. It set a tone that Deeya had not fully expected, a tone of zero lies, zero secrets. It made her wonder what exactly she knew about Deeya....

She spoke as she reached the halfway point of the carpeted dais saying, "Ah, there you are, El'Mindeeya. I had expected you earlier, I was going to show you the gardens."

Deeya rose to her feet and bowed slightly saying, "I'm sorry, Your Grace, I was busy in town. I had to tear myself away from all of it to come here. That, and I did not realize you had wanted to do such a thing. I'm sorry for the inconvenience."

Ryn'Vey sat at the other side of the table with an almost perplexed look and Deeya followed suit knowing that the perplexed look was Ryn'Vey wondering why her magic had not compulsed Deeya to arrive earlier. Ryn'Vey then ordered them both a bottle of red wine from the three servants who had followed her into the room.

The servants were dressed in drab, modest clothing. The young woman had a bow strapped to her back, along with a short sword. The two men both had a long sword on their back. In the Duke's castle, the servants were part of the guard, in a way. From what Deeya understood from the rumor mill was that the weapons were more for show than anything else, though Deeya wondered.

The wine itself was not a handful of meters from the table, so the taller servant just had to get it and start pouring. Deeya knew a bit about vintages and believed the bottle would be expensive, but then she expected no less from the start of this meeting than an overt display of power.

"So, what brought the Emerald Bard to this small city," Ryn'Vey asked as the servant poured the deep red wine into ornate glasses. The wine's bouquet spread quickly, revealing it to be very flavorful. Deeya reached for her glass and said, "I'm a wandering minstrel, I go where the wind takes me and play where I can." She then sipped the wine carefully. It never mattered that she consumed a potion earlier and laid down magics that would resist any poison or magical taint, eating someone's more than likely poisoned food was not easy. She made a pleased face at drinking the wine that she let slide through her lips without tasting and said, "In the end, I was just passing through. I played a gig at the Deal at the Crossroads and was headed west before I headed to the Port of Nails."

Deeya met gazes with the elf's blue eyed gaze. It was hard not to see Ash in that face, then she would make a face and the resemblance would vanish. Ryn'Vey's face was hard to read that way, though, as the expressions from Ashengrey's was so different that it was easy to confuse one look for another. If Deeya had to guess, the emotion currently being conveyed by her face was a look of triumph, as she said, "So, nothing else brought you here? Not even, perhaps, a lover?"

Triumph it was. She did know things outside of what Deeya wanted her to know. But was she talking about Ashengrey? The bard played coy, "I no longer take lovers. It was a foolish thing to do in my youth, luckily I grew out of such folly."

Ryn'Vey leaned back and sniffed before saying, "No more games, Bard. I know you are here because my daughter contacted you somehow. I've had you followed all around the city since we knew you were here, but you've not been seen at her house or where we keep her."

So many things revealed all at once. Deeya's mind raced through it all but stuck on one single tidbit. She knew she had been followed, she wondered if they knew she had a connection to Ashengrey, but screaming above it all, was a single question, "Daughter?"

Ryn'Vey gave Deeya a look of exhaustion, "Look, the time for playing the fool is over. I swear, if I didn't need Ashengrey I'd have killed her. But you on the other hand, you have many agendas here, and all of them interfere with what I'm trying to accomplish."

Ryn'Vey pushed her empty food tray away, towards Deeya, yet Deeya noticed that the servants did not move. They only stood there with a blank face. Deeya controlled her face, and took her first, and last, sip of red wine. Maybe it was good wine after all….

"Nothing to say, El'Mindeeya? We elves never age, but I saw you die before, I'll see you die again."

With all the different options there were for this trap, Deeya never expected something so overt. Seduction, using her magic, the fact that she looked like Ash, and even surprise came to mind far before the idea of watching her extend her arm with the three servants watching. The air around Deeya began to heat up, and she felt her hair start to stand on end; *Electricity…. Good.* Deeya stood up and opened her mouth. From that mouth came words, sang in a certain key, and the electricity forming around her simply fizzled out. The last bit of electricity dissipated before Ryn'Vey's eyes as the bard stood to her full height. Ryn'Vey's expression was comical, the best word was describe it was: incredulous. Deeya then simply shouted at Ryn'Vey.

The force of the sonic blast pushed Ryn'Vey across the room and bounced her forcibly off the far wall. Deeya noticed that Ryn'Vey's dress had partially shredded from the force of the sonic blast, as she landed hard on the floor, seemingly unconscious. Deeya leapt over the table and drew her axe, while missing her sword. Between her and the unconscious Ryn'Vey stood the three servants that were now drawing their own weapons to defend their mistress.

Deeya started singing a song as she attacked the three. To those witnessing it, her movements seemed to quicken, yet to herself, time seemed to slow. The song did not actually quicken her movements, but made her able to react faster. She blocked and parried the blows, trying hard not to kill the servants. Deep inside she knew their brains did not belong to themselves anymore. Ryn'Vey was a powerful magic user and could twist and shape anyone's will to her own. After punching one servant hard enough in the face to knock the man unconscious, Deeya ducked under a strike then kicked the striking woman in the face, all the while parrying yet another blow. She was fluid and fast, and soon she was standing amongst the three unconscious bodies of Ryn'Vey's servants, all before a fireball slammed into her chest.

She was launched several feet in the air, landing hard on her back, her axe sliding away from her.

"Truly, Bard? You wield the magic of the Goddess of Music? When we first met, centuries from now, you did nothing of the sort. You were just some silly singer who helped my lover and I raise Ashengrey. What has my spawn done to your timeline to make you so powerful? First, I was going to kill you, but now... now I must possess you and this power you have."

Deeya listened to the Ryn'Vey's rant as the deadly blond elf with the shredded dress, that barely kept her modest, slowly, confidently walked towards the downed bard. After the woman was done talking, Deeya rolled onto her belly and struggled to push herself up to her knees, all the while, facing away from the sorceress. At the mention of Ashengrey's name Deeya felt the inevitable tendrils try to push into her brain, and she started whispering a song.

Ryn'Vey continued her slow stride towards the kneeling bard, with the shredded gown clinging in uneven swaths, she looked like something out of a fever dream, beautiful and terrifying all at once. The spell seemed to be taking effect, as she watched the tendrils crawl into Deeya's short hair, digging into the bard's brain. Ryn'Vey smiled to herself triumphantly. When she stepped within a handful of meters from the bard, a shrill screech assaulted Ryn'Vey's ears. It was an ear-splitting painful sound that even caused her vision to skew. She had never heard such a sound. It caused her not to hear the soft clicking that shortly preceded a soft "thwap" sound, which preceded an arrow protruding from between her breasts.

Ryn'Vey fell to the ground, clutching the arrow with one hand, while her mind scrambled to escape. She held her other hand above her head and said two or three words, before another arrow entered below her chin and poked its tip beyond the hair on her head....

Deeya stood above the dead body of Ryn'Vey, her green clothes ripped and torn from the short battle, blood seeping from the burns on her arm. The green lacquered, metallic bow she held clicked softly as it folded back up into a small box with a clip that fit neatly on her belt.

Just as Deeya expected, the entire castle was roused in an instant. Ryn'Vey's mind control was broken and pandemonium was ensuing. Deeya knew that she could escape, if she so chose, but this was a problem she had to deal with herself. The duke himself was one of the first people to run into the dining hall to see Deeya standing above the woman who had controlled his mind into thinking that she was his mother, even though she had actually been his advisor, who turned into his lover and his captor. He realized, in that moment, the Emerald Bard had freed them all from the evil woman's spell. The rest, Deeya had to explain to him. He issued the orders he knew he had to order, as his mind had been foggy for well over a month.

It was then, during all the chaos that quickly ensued, that Deeya realized that Ashengrey had been the man's advisor before Ryn'Vey had taken over the position. That took some explaining as well, as Deeya was still unsure about the sister/daughter angle. She went with Ash's story, about Ryn'Vey being her sister. A twin made far more sense.

Later, after Ash had been taken from the prison, she was shown, in private, to the Duke beside the corpse. Deeya was being held separate at the time, a prisoner of the room she was taken to inside the castle. Later still, Deeya was ushered into the throne room where the

Duke sat upon his throne. The official discussion over what had happened was finally beginning, yet Ashengrey was nowhere to be seen. Deeya played with her cards close to her chest, meaning she stuck to a story and never deviated.

She was a simple traveling minstrel looking for work. Ashengrey had contacted her before she was taken to prison to request help. Deeya had spent the time trying to figure out what was even going on. Deeya was obviously being trapped by Ryn'Vey when the fight broke out. Ryn'Vey cast magic like crazy everywhere, while Deeya scampered for help. It was Ryn'Vey, in the story, which knocked out her own servants by accident, and Deeya used a nearby bow to slay Ryn'Vey while she was distracted. It was a case of extreme luck that Deeya was able to prevail.

The Duke listened to the story and nodded. Officials stood all around her, listening as well. Finally, after the tale was told, the Duke finished nodding, and motioned for the bard to step aside. She sat upon the steps up to the raised dais which the throne stood upon. The officials argued this way and that way, trying to gain favor for this or that. In the end, the Duke listened to the wise few who understood the story and what they were even there for.

Finally, in walked Ashengrey A'Taril. She had bathed and been clothed with extra clothes people had available within the castle. It was a shock to see her looking herself but not wearing her regular style of clothing. She normally wore a robe style of dress, flowing blue and gold. She normally looked like a sorceress. She wore a loose dark brown top, which looked as if it were a poor woman's blouse, along with light brown cloth pants with miss matched colored boots. Her hair was done up in a bun and she wore no jewelry. The beggar-like clothes were ill fitting and looked uncomfortable, but they hid all signs of any abuse she may have suffered within the prison.

Despite all of that, she strode down the carpet that lined the middle of the throne room like a queen and knelt before the Duke like a humble aristocrat. He bid her rise and she stood. Her eyes never left him as she said, "Your Highness, I am sure the Emerald Bard filled you in on most of the story."

Deeya, who was still sitting to the side, on the steps, spoke up, saying, "Only what I understood.... Which wasn't much...."

Duke Quinlan seemed to ignore Deeya, for the most part, even though he nodded and said, "For the most part. Apparently, this...woman, whom you call your sister, took over your guise, and enthralled us all with some sorcery?"

Ashengrey nodded, "That would be the long and short of it."

Duke Quinlan sighed, "How can I ever look at my wife without shame?"

It had become very apparent, as their conversation went on, that Ryn'Vey had taken Duke Quinlan as a lover and forced him to banish his own wife to the dungeons. There she had undergone several mistreatments at the hand of the enthralled duke. From all accounts it was a horror from which she would not soon recover. In that fashion, since Ryn'Vey looked exactly like Ashengrey, Ash was going to have to leave the city. The meeting itself was cut off after a fair amount of time due to a message that a representative from the King would be there in the morning.

The decision was quickly made to sequester everyone involved separately for the night. For Deeya, the concept was sheer torture, as there were so many things she needed to discuss with Ashengrey, but she knew the time would eventually come. That night she worked on her music, writing songs and lyrics.

On the next day, Deeya got a glance at the damage to the dining room. The curtain separated the raised platform from the main dining area was in tatters, the table and chairs Deeya had sat in with Ryn'Vey were mere splinters, and the carpet had huge burn holes. Not to mention the dark red stains that were strewn everywhere. She was amazed at how much damage was caused by such a small, quick fight, but such is the damage magic can do. It was no wonder that so many people feared it.

During those early hours, Deeya only caught glimpses of Ashengrey, as she was being escorted around without much leeway with what she was doing. Deeya learned through her listening to whispers that the special envoy was arriving at noon to handle the situation. And unfortunately, she had an idea who it might be....

Noon came and Deeya stood in the throne room with several minor officials. Duke Quinlan sat upon his throne, with his head in his hands, trying to pull himself together. He had controlled himself moderately during the meeting the night before, but now...now he seemed beyond devastated. It was almost like the memories of what he had done under the command of the sorceress,

Ryn'Vey, had come trickling back to him slowly, throughout the night. Ashengrey, who stood at his side, cleared her throat, and repeated the words that the duke had missed due to his sobbing, "Duke Quinlan, this is Prince Kell."

Deeya recognized the man the instant she'd seen him, even though their last meeting had taken place in a darkened corner of a darkened bar. The duke looked up, trying to focus through bleary eyes, and said, "Prince Kell, as you can see, my House is in disarray at the moment, I am sorry I could not receive you with more courtesy."

Condar Kell was a tall, proud man, whom Deeya knew better than she wished she did. He had shockingly dark red, short hair with a short bright red beard. His eyes were piercingly brown and sharp. He stood in front of the duke with a smirk, knowing that he had the situation well in hand. Deeya stood slightly behind and to the right of the Prince, while Ashengrey stood almost directly in front of her. It was hard to pay attention, as Ash was pleasantly lit by the artificial light of torches and candles that lit the throne's dais. Kell replied in his very stately voice, a voice very different from the one Deeya had heard the night before she got into the city of Norvale, "Do not worry about courtesy, I am fully aware of the situation that occurred here, and I am here to offer the support of the crown, should you request it of me."

Deeya held her breath, because Ryn'Vey had held his mind for some time, and she was worried that his mind had come to accept the prejudices that she had planted in his mind. It was hard to accept help when your mind was clouded against any form of help offered.

Duke Quinlan nodded quickly though, and said, "Aye, I do believe I could use some assistance. My mind...it does not still feel right, and it turns out the witch's influence went far beyond just me."

Deeya had not expected that part, but it was true, the woman had taken just about every servant in the castle under her spell, and most of the guardsmen. She had no clue how strong that type of magic could be, part of her even wondered what Ash was capable of, but the thought would not take seed as she could smell Ash's scent wafting down to her, and that turned her thoughts away from anything...evil....

Kell bowed respectfully to the Duke and said, "I shall handle this all myself, and we will restore your name as best we can."

Prince Kell, Ashengrey, and the duke all retired to an antechamber to discuss terms. When they walked out, the Duke was in reasonably better spirits. Ashengrey and Prince Kell walked up to Deeya, who had been waiting by the doors. Kell said, "We will not forget how you helped here, El'Mindeeya, your debt has been paid to the crown. Please come to the capital and settle things with my Uncle, the King."

Deeya bowed respectfully to Kell as he took his leave of Ash and Deeya. Ash quickly took the opportunity to steer herself and Deeya to a balcony overlooking the courtyard of the castle. Ash still had on the borrowed brown clothing from the night before. Some of the bruises that were hidden under the garb were starting to spread to visible areas and she obviously still felt uncomfortable with all that had happened. "What now, Bard?"

Deeya sighed and looked out over the city, "Same as always, I continue walking through the world."

"No, Bard, I mean right now."

Deeya sighed and said, "I have my stuff stored at your home.

Ashengrey shook her head, "What makes me want to believe there is not much left of my "home?""

Deeya grimaced. "Yeah, I've seen worse. It made a good base for me to operate out of."

Ash looked at Deeya. "You stayed there for all of this?" she asked incredulously.

Deeya smirked at the blonde elf and said, "The first night was the worst…."

Ash laid a hand on the bard's shoulder and said, "I think I can understand that…. The night after your visit was the worst night in the cell…."

Deeya closed her eyes and simply felt her former lover's hand on her shoulder. It felt natural, it felt *right*. It was the smallest of things, but as they say…those were the things that mean the most. Deeya let the hand rest there, the simple point of contact was very real, and very grounding.

"We should go there," Deeya said softly, trying not to let emotion seep into her voice. "So, I can take care of those bruises and get my stuff."

Ash then said, "And talk before you leave."

Deeya did not reply to the statement that sounded like something between a plea and a question. Instead, she patted the hand on her shoulder, stood up from the railing of the balcony, and walked back through the castle.

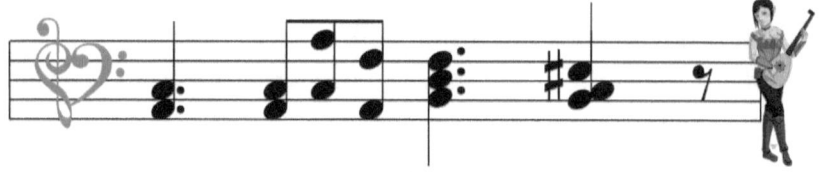

Movement 3: Old Wounds

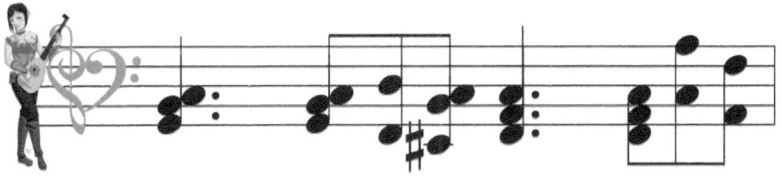

As the two female elves walked back to the Avenue of White, they found themselves surrounded by an air of silence. There was so much the two needed to talk about, yet neither wanted to start the coming conversation in public. As excruciating as the silence was, the steps up to Ash's mansion were the worst part.

As soon as Ash shut the door behind them, Deeya said, "I suppose you'll miss this city."

Ash looked around at the chaos of her former home and said, "It was a good home base. I had known that Ryn'Vey was operating here, but I had no clue as to what extent."

Deeya sighed, looking around at the remnants of Ash's home. "What will you do next?"

Ash sighed as well, shrugged off the shawl she wore, threw it on a random pile of mess, and said, "There is no telling, now that she is dead for sure." She could not help adding, "I hope at least." She then walked past Deeya while saying, "I am just glad there is nothing left for me here." Ash then pushed off a pile of stuff from her sofa, sat down in the newly vacated spot, and continued, "I found that Ryn'Vey was working with the Kells. They planted her here for some reason. I can't tell if she took control with their permission, by their command, or if she did it on her own."

Deeya stood over Ash, and lifted the blond elf's sleeves, and inspected the bruises on Ash's forearms. She peeked down Ash's back to see the cuts and bruises from the lashings she had taken. "It would not surprise me, decades ago I had a run in with them. Needless to say, I've incurred some old debts with them I've never repaid."

Ash winced at having her clothing moved on her wounds, even though her heart was beating faster from being examined by the bard, and said, "So that's what the Prince was talking to you about? You going to go?"

It's a trap, I have to go, especially after the mess I had getting in here...."

"Deeya, I'm sorry." Her voice was painfully sincere. It carried a weight of regret far beyond knowing what Deeya had to explain and keep her cover as 'just a bard.' There was only so much that could be explained by sheer luck. Deeya was convincing, even though she was barely hurt from all the devastation that she said Ryn'Vey along had unleashed.

Deeya, though, had other things on her mind, other pains. She stepped back from Ash, looked down at the sitting elf and point blank asked her, "How much older are you? Since we last met, I mean?"

Ash slumped over as she heaved a heavy sigh, "I've had to travel, Deeya."

Deeya shook her head, knowing that Ash dropped the *time* from her 'travel.' "How long has it been for you?"

Ash looked up at Deeya, tears welling in her eyes, "I honestly do not know anymore, but I would suspect, since we left the college, four hundred years, give or take a decade."

Deeya made a face and rubbed her right eye with her right hand. She finally let go of the expression and ran her hand through her short hair. There were so many questions she knew not to ask. She wanted to know how many times that Ash had met Deeya in the future, if their relationship was somehow going to be repaired, or if it truly was in tatters forever. Maybe they never spoke again after this, or maybe they were married.

Ashengrey had indeed traveled throughout the future, and she knew the answer to every question inside Deeya's head. She ached to tell the bard, yet she knew she could not. Both elves, in that very moment, hated Ash's ability to time travel the exact same amount.

Deeya finally let go of those questions and asked the one she knew she had to ask to get real answers. "Ryn'Vey was not your sister, was she?"

Ash nodded and looked off into the distance, "Deeya, I once told you how I am from the future...."

Deeya cut her off, "And that you have changed things here in this time so that you will never be born, yes, I know this story...."

"But what you do not know...." Ash sighed, heavily. She then took a deep breath, looked Deeya in the eyes, and told the bard for the first time what she had only told one other person in all her time of traveling, "Ryn'Vey created me by magical means. In that other time stream, she caused the destruction of the world, and only survived it by...well, making a copy of herself, implanting the embryo into a woman she knew who raised me as her child, then that Ryn'Vey and I together used our magic to send me back in time. At least, at the time I thought it was only me...."

"So, she's neither your sister, nor your mother as she claims, but both at the same time?" Deeya shook her head, sat down on a pile of destroyed something or other beside Ash on the couch, and muttered, "I hate time travel."

"Deeya, the first time I met a version of you, you were almost three thousand years old, and you died in my arms, after having saved my life." A tear formed in Ash's eye and ran down her cheek as she spoke, "When you first met me, I had just traveled back in time, and I think part of what I felt for you was because of what the alternate future you did...."

Deeya stood up, shaking her head, "Just stop, just...stop." Deeya took a few strides from Ash and said, "I don't care about time travel, and I don't care about this or that, all I know is I loved you, and I wasn't there when you needed me."

Ash rose from her seat and approached Deeya from behind. She reached out and put her hand on Deeya's back and whispered, "I'm so sorry, I should not have put that much pressure on you."

Deeya wanted to shrug off Ash's hand, but it felt too right. She simply let herself be comforted by the small touch as Ashengrey continued, "I did not know I'd need...." She then retracted her hand during the pause and whispered, "Need someone to rescue me then and there." Deeya turned around and looked at the beautiful blonde elf as tears started to leak out of her blue eyes. "Ryn'Vey was ready for me when I came for her. I thought I had surprise on my side, that she did not know I was after her, but she had just been defeated. Another me had been captured and was being tortured to get information. That future version of me was rescued by my mom. Ryn'Vey came at me with a vengeance, and...and...."

Deeya stepped forward and curled her arms around the crying beauty. Ash sobbed into her shoulder. After a few moments of tears she whispered, "I had no idea she even knew I existed.... She almost killed me and I simply used my power to go to the one place I knew you'd be."

"And I wasn't there," Deeya said softly.

Ash shook her head, pushed away from Deeya, but winced as the movement hurt her wounds.

Deeya sighed and unwrapped her arms. "Look, let's heal you first."

Ash nodded and followed the bard into her bedroom. Deeya knew two different healing songs. One was just a broad song, the one she used the most. She sang it and those who could hear it simply healed faster, whether it was cuts or bruises. Yet that song was limited, it took time for a large amount of injuries. The other song, it was more targeted, and she had to sing it directly into wounds. When she first started using it, needless to say, she felt a bit silly. Honestly, to this day it was still a bit awkward. Especially when she had to ask, "Are you wearing undergarments?"

Ash nodded her head indicating a yes, even though she looked a bit timid. Deeya then said, "Can you strip down to them?"

Ash turned her back to the bard, facing the bed, which she was standing at the foot of. The bed had been used and remade. In fact, Ash noticed, before she felt awkward again, the bedroom was the neatest room in the house, almost as if Deeya had cleaned it just a bit. She then unbuckled the belt that held on her breeches. All of the clothing she currently wore was not hers. It all fit her badly and she was happy to get out of them, even if it was during this situation.

Deeya tried to watch stoically, but she could not help but feel her blood warm to the eroticism of the situation. Ash let the breeches fall to the floor around her ankles. Bruises blossomed from underneath her modest undershorts, down the back of her thighs all the way to her knees, which were highlighted by a multitude of cuts. The expanse of skin, along with the ruin of it, took Deeya's breath away. How Ash sat down, Deeya did not know.

Ash then pulled the loose, ill-fitting shirt off of herself. In honesty, to Deeya, it appeared as though the motion was a slow languid reveal of alabaster skin. Familiar skin, once kissed and caressed in laughter and quiet, now marred by cuts and silent groans of pain. As she tossed the garment aside Deeya realized that Ash was not wearing underclothes on her upper body.

Ash was glad that her back was to Deeya, as her face was glowing red. Her body ached for Deeya's touch, but she knew the touch she wanted was not going to come. She knew Deeya would not allow it, as the bard was still too hurt, over so many things that she knew she was going to hear about very soon.

"Oh, Ash...," Deeya lamented before she started singing. Ash had felt Deeya's song before, many times. She thought back to the first time as she felt the warm breath and pleasant vibrations coming from lips that were so very close to her bare skin....

They had been in the college; they had met there. Deeya was researching old bards, Ash had just arrived and was looking for how to save the world, trying to understand what went wrong to cause the devastation of the future from which she came. She had known that other Deeya in the other timeline had been a friend she had grown up with, almost a sister. She knew that this Deeya was different from the moment she saw the bard. First off, she was younger, by centuries. Secondly, she held a power that the other timeline Deeya did not. Deeya was the marker that made her realize that there was something far different in this timeline than there was in the other. She had wanted to avoid all vestiges from that other life. There were four elves that existed in that other life that existed now, one of them was the elf that had carried Ash in her womb. Ash knew, at the time, she was not going to go there at all.

When El'Mindeeya approached her in the library, Ash got a taste of how different she really was. The bard made the seemingly simple request of having Ash accompany her to an old dwarven cave system close by a town Ash needed to go to anyways. Ash had thought, "Why not?"

It turned into a harrowing adventure that ended with a death-defying leap off a cliff into the waters below. They made it to a beach down the shoreline where she lost her virginity to the Emerald Bard in a beautiful night of passion.

Deeya stood up behind her and said, "Done." The bard looked over her work, Ash's skin looked as pristine as it had that night on that beach, oh so long ago. "Flawless."

Ash could not help herself, the memory of that night, the feeling of being so close to nude with the female elf she had known in a lovingly carnal way, she turned around. She looked Deeya in the eyes. With those big, deep wells of blue eyes. With an expression that screamed at the bard to take her now. To rip off those white panties and do things with that melodic mouth that could compose the most beautiful ballads.

But Deeya never looked at her face. Her gaze saw more of Ash than she meant to, despite how careful she was attempting to be. Old aches flared back to life, coupled with memories of caressing, kissing, and so many other things lovers do but can't put to modest words. Instead of stepping forward like her body urged her to, she turned away. She forced herself to walk to the closet and pull out a loose shirt, tossing it in Ash's general direction.

The red-faced Ashengrey caught the loose shirt and slipped it on, over her head. "Okay, I'm decent."

Deeya stepped back out of the closet. Even now, with a battered grace, wearing a loose shirt, she was the shape of every memory Deeya had worked so hard to forget. The shirt hung off of her right shoulder, falling down to about mid-bicep, and barely covered half of her belly.

A comfortable shirt to sleep in on a hot night.

She tried not to look, to let her eyes linger, but the glimpse of bare skin, the softness, the familiarity... t twisted something inside her she wasn't ready to sing about. In her mind's eye, she saw the woman as she'd once known her. Vulnerable, powerful, too beautiful to resist.... Long before those memories and visions weren't tinged with a pain.

No, those days were gone.

"I should go," Deeya managed to say, still not able to meet Ash's eyes.

Ash frowned and said, "No, wait...."

Deeya picked up her pack, out of the hidden compartment she had been hiding it in. Without looking at the blonde woman she was trying to deny she was in love with, she said, "I was supposed to be at a gig two weeks ago, Ash. I've got a life to live, so do you."

Ash sighed, "Look, I'm sorry for that letter. I was hurt. I was a young girl in love, and I lashed out. And I never knew why you were not there."

Deeya looked Ash in the eyes. The bard's green eyes were full of...depth. So many emotions playing together. It made her hard to read. When Deeya pointed out, "You never asked," Ash did not know if it was said in anger, pain, sadness, or any other type of emotion such a thing could be said.

Ash broke eye contact and looked at her own feet. "I never asked because I thought I had no right to ask."

Deeya sat her pack on the floor, undid her axe from the holster on her hip, and held it up for Ash to see, while she asked, "Do you know what this is?"

The blade was, as it had always been when Ash had seen it in the future, a tomahawk like blade, with a curved hilt connected to a beautifully forged blade shaped like a Treble and Bass clef combined into a single symbol. When held upright, the Bass Clef curve made the front of the blade, one could perceive that the two symbols formed a heart.

Ash shook her head, always thinking that the axe's symbol just meant the love of music, making her blonde hair play around her face, "I just know it is your axe...."

Deeya then hummed softly. The blade began to softly glow. Then two circles appeared on the outside of the symbol, completing the bass cleft symbol. Ash's eyes opened wide. Deeya stopped humming, the blade dimmed back to shiny steel, and the bard said, "Do you remember when we laid on that beach after making love and wondered about the gods above?"

Ash blushed and nodded.

Deeya simply continued without noticing, "Well, this is the Sonnetic Axe. It is a gift from the Goddess of Music, Sonnet. It contains just a pinch of the destructive power of music." Deeya looked into Ashengrey's eyes, "The Goddess chose me, and I had to go on a great quest, just as I was leaving to come to our meeting point. In fact, the day I was supposed to meet you, I was standing on top of the Mountain of Death, speaking with what I can only describe as an Angel."

Ash's eyes got big, "An Angel?" Her voice was barely a breath of a whisper.

Deeya then said, "It was a man wearing not but a fabric loin cloth. He was beyond beautiful, he was perfect. And he had wings, Ash." Deeya's eyes started tearing up at the memory. "Wings that were so very big." And then Deeya's eyes looked deep into Ashengrey's. "His voice was music, and his message was a song only I could hear."

Ash looked at Deeya with her mouth agape. Finally, she tried to stammer out a phrase, but all that came out was, "El'Mindeeya Do'Katal, the Emerald Bard, Scion of Music, and Avatar of Sonnet, the Goddess of Song."

Deeya holstered the axe, picked up her backpack, shouldered it, and said, "Goodbye, Ash."

Ash grabbed Deeya's arm as she tried to walk by. She said, "Bard, wait...I...." Deeya's emerald eyes looked up into Ash's deep blue, and she leaned in to kiss Deeya.

Deeya recoiled.

"No Ash, I cannot kiss you, not now, not ever again, not after how you treated me that day.... Not after the lie of you killing Ryn'Vey before."

Ash literally growled, "Damnit, Bard. I didn't know about this, about your quest, even in the future you've never told that story...."

Deeya's head did not turn to look at Ash. Deeya just stared at the floor in front of as her words slowly bled from her lips. "So, we meet again in the future?" Even though it was a question, Deeya seemed to say it more like a statement.

"Look here, you green wearing ass, Ryn'Vey almost killed me. And you know what?" Deeya turned to look at Ash, and saw the genuine anger. Deeya took a step back from the elf. She was fired up and venting. Deeya knew what she could do with magic as well. If Ash got mad enough the entire city could wind up as the middle of a fireball. "I was a flying fool. That night, under the stars, on that beach, I fell so madly in love with you that I knew that I would do anything to be with you." She stepped forward, pointing a finger at Deeya's chest. "In fact, I made the dumbest mistake that I have ever made then or since. I went after Ryn'Vey as quickly as I could to keep her from coming after you."

Without knowing it, Deeya had backed against the wall. She dropped her pack to get further way from the advancing blonde beauty, "Our fight will cause what people will believe to be a natural disaster in another decade." She finally reached Deeya and poked the finger right between Deeya's breasts, "I cut her head off myself. I might have been bleeding from burns and wounds all over, but I had more of her blood on me than I had of my own. Only the thought of you kept me standing. Only the thought of you gave me the strength to cast one last spell. And after I cast that spell, with what I worried was my dying breath...I arrived to find you were not there."

Deeya stayed silent as Ash continued her ranting vent, her back flush against the wall. She looked as if she was ready to level the city, but then it all changed. "I was devastated, I was crushed, and yes, after I survived my wounds, I wrote you a letter designed to hurt you as badly as I had been hurt. Was my hurt justified? No. Was it worth it? No. Did I even care why you weren't there? Not at the time.

"Then I left. I left for good. I traveled as far as I could. I tested my powers. And then one day...." She took her poking finger away and turned away from Deeya, "I came across your daughter."

Deeya took a step forward, the change in tone made her want to reach out and comfort Ash, but she dare not, as Ash kept going, "Mindee was old. She was gardening, of all things. She looked at me with a wonderful smile and waved. She invited me in for tea. And she told me things…."

Deeya interjected, "Spoilers, as you call them?"

Ash nodded, turning her side towards Deeya, "I'm not going to tell you what she said, but…."

"We're going to kiss again?"

Ash looked into Deeya's green eyes and said, "Yes."

Deeya sighed and sat down at the end of the bed. "I'm guessing it's not going to be any time soon." Deeya ran her fingers through her short black hair and said, "I know you say you killed her, but I just did…."

Ash sat next to Deeya on the bed, "I understand about kissing." She put her hand on Deeya's knee and said, "But honestly, I don't know how she survived. I don't know if she found out about me killing her and changed the timeline. For all I know she could have escaped her body somehow or there could be two of her."

Deeya rolled her eyes, "Two? Like the one that traveled back and the one that was already there when she did?"

Ash's expression turned introspective, "Actually…you may have a point…."

"Did you know ahead of time that I was going to face her here and kill her?"

Ash picked up her feet and hugged her knees to herself as she looked at Deeya and said, "No, but…after what had happened to me, I hoped you would. I knew you were the only one that could...."

Deeya stood up, "I'm sure you remember my story, of my first love?"

Ash nodded and looked sullen. "Yes, and I know you feel lied to and used. It's not something you can easily get over. It's part of you, since you were abused. It's a trauma that you will deal with for the rest of your long, elven life."

Deeya nodded, "I'm glad you know why I can't kiss you and why I need to leave."

Ash stood up. "Deeya," she said, taking the bard's hand, "I swear to you, I will never again use you, or lie to you, or keep secrets that will harm you. I have not done so this time, nor will I in my past or future."

Deeya grinned slightly. There was no hate in her heart, no harm done, but the wounds of it all were still too fresh, she had to go. She took her hand out of Ash's and put in on Ash's cheek. "For the record, I fell in love that night as well."

Ash grinned and nuzzled into the bard's strong, yet soft hand. "I know."

El'Mindeeya took one last look at Ashengrey as she stood there, vulnerable in a way Deeya remembered all too well. The soft shirt hanging loose, the lines of her, the familiar fall of golden hair, the scent of brimstone and lavender, the sadness tucked behind a simple smile, the aching echo of all they had once been.... She was beautiful, and Deeya could not bear looking into those beautiful blue eyes any longer. Deeya took her hand away, and said, "Goodbye, Ash, may your Journey be worth the Travels."

Ashengrey smiled weakly and said, "Goodbye, my beautiful bard, may music herald your footsteps, and may the Goddess of Music sing your praises to the stars."

They hugged briefly, both smelling each other's hair, both relishing in the feel of the other's body up against their own, before Deeya walked out the door. Ash stopped her briefly and said, "Sorry, one quick question, before Ryn'Vey died, was she chanting a spell?"

Deeya's eyes look saddened, "Yes, before I finished her off with an arrow through her chin."

In silence, the bard turned, walked out of the house, onto the street, and onward into her own future. Ash knew that most of what Deeya was feeling was because she had to kill people, and if some people learned of it, it would ruin her facade of being a meek little Bard. But then, Ash also knew what was about to happen to Deeya, what she was walking into with the Kells. But she also knew Deeya would come out stronger than she went into it....

Ashengrey, herself, had her own issues to take care of. That day when she beheaded Ryn'Vey, Ryn'Vey had been chanting as well. Deeya might have been onto something with the two different versions of Ryn'Vey, but...was there a spell that could evacuate someone out of a body before that body was killed?

She ran through her destroyed home gathering everything she needed. Her blue traveling clothes, which fit her upper body snuggly, with divided skirts on the lower half of her. She then went to the tree in the dining room, the same that had held a note for Deeya. She jerked the tree out of the pot and as she did, it changed. A second later, instead of an uprooted tree, she held her staff, which amplified her magic, and the pot it had been in had turned into a travel bag.

The contents of her bag were strewn about all over, some hidden by the same illusionary spells as the bag and staff so no one could tell the whole was important. When it was all combined again, she went to the middle of her living room. She chanted a word and tapped her staff on the floor. All of the debris from her life, and all the furniture was shoved away from her, some of it shattering as it impacted the walls of the room.

She then drew a design on the floor in front of her with the end of her staff and chanted four words. Yellow lights flashed all around her, a wind came up, blowing all manner of everything every single direction, and she lifted up off the floor. The design she drew onto the floor turned into a puff of smoke, which then flourished into a column of smoke, twisting from the floor to the ceiling. The smoke swirled and swirled around the floating elven mage. She continued the chant, even though the wind blowing around the room made it impossible for her to even hear herself. Suddenly the smoke column that twisted around her changed. It shifted, turning into individual rings that ringed the blonde elven mage eight times in a sphere, which then collapsed in upon itself, shrinking Ash, the smoke, and the lights out of existence. All that was left was the dust and debris that collided upon the point where the spell and the elf had vanished, which then slowly settled back onto the room's floor.

--

A single candle flickered on top of the desk as Prince Condar Kell finished his letter. Deep within Duke Quinlan's castle, the prince reread his letter to his Uncle. He could read the code itself, laying the groundwork for the trap that would destroy the "famed" Emerald Bard. She had shown her true colors here, shedding the façade of being a simple bard and proving she was indeed a deadly elven spy....

Elves believed they should rule the world, since they were eternal beings. It was time they were stopped, once and for all. Every stop that had ever been applied to a race, though, needed a start. And who better to start with than their most prolific and well-regarded spy. It was time to bury all of El'Mindeeya Do'Katal's lies and secrets, alongside her damnable lithe elven body.

After going over the words, encoded and not, he folded the parchment, held the stick of wax up to the candle flame, and dabbed the parchment fold. He then took his signet ring and pressed it into the bead of wax. As he pulled the ring away, he admired the Seal of House Kell. Many years ago, the Emerald Bard had been involved in the fall of both the prince's father and the prince's grandfather. Both had sat upon the throne, both were removed, leaving him not sitting upon the throne....

He turned the parchment over and inscribed the name of his Uncle, the current reigning King Kell. It was time to take his revenge. Revenge against her schemes, revenge against meddling elves, and revenge against the destruction of Ryn'Vey and his plans in Norvale....

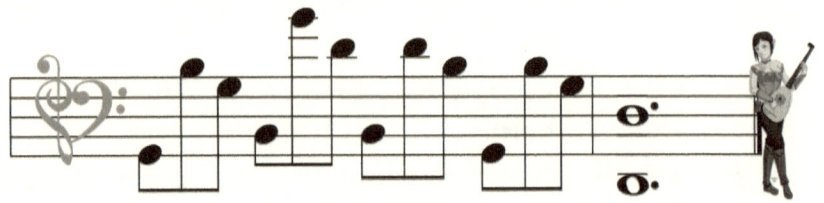

3: The Sonata of Buried Secrets

Movement 1: A Mistake with Consequences

The throne room was dark. The torches were too high up and the ceiling was too dark to reflect any good light. Most throne rooms were always well lit, to display the splendor of the monarch who sat upon the regal chair at the end.

Not this throne room, not this monarch.

It had been a long time since Deeya had set foot in this particular throne room.

Not long enough, though.

She remembered it quite differently then. King Leland Kell sat upon the throne that day, Leland VII, if Deeya remembered it correctly....

The castle itself was one of the wonders of the human world. Located on the cliffs high above a vast lake, parts of the structure looked to have been carved out of the stone itself. There was no city surrounding the castle, it stood at the end of the road from the capital city of the Kell Kingdom, which was sadly named Kell. There was a massive cave system below the castle where water, cold and hot, ran in streams. This unique geological feature gave the castle an advantage over every castle in the world, as it was almost self-sustaining. They just needed to import food. The first Kells built the castle with the help of some of the greatest magic users that had ever existed.

The Kell name bore a long dynasty, tracing back long before maybe even Deeya's parents were born. They were a proud lot, as this country was ruled by a direct descendent of the man that first united the land, and was the oldest stable country on the mainland, meaning they hardly ever had to change their borders or names, like so many countries in existence. In the end, some people are never content with what they have....

Leland VII's youngest child, King Edward Kell was sitting on his throne and honestly this was the first time Deeya had ever laid eyes on the human. He was a portly man, filling his grand throne, while picking his teeth with a knight from a chess set. His beard was long and braided, and very black. Deeya could see his grey hair under his crown and deduced that he dyed the beard. Considering there was a dwarven contingent in his country trying to mine a mountain, she figured he was just trying to show off.

The King tried to hide his disgust of Deeya as she walked towards him with Prince Condar Kell flanking her, but Deeya could see it in his brown eyes. She had seen that disgust from so many humans, bigotry is easy to spot when you have fallen under its disgusting gaze so many times.

The prince beside her, she knew far too well. He had warned her that entering Duke Quinlan's province would have consequences. He had been the first to "greet" her upon entering the country, in a dark part of a shady saloon like inn. There he had reminded her that she was not supposed to be in the country at all due to the King's own orders. Later, though, after Deeya had helped Duke Quinlan with the whole mind-controlling sorceress thing, Prince Condar Kell had promised that this would help clear her name and debts to the Kell crown.

So here they were, striding towards the King. The Emerald Bard was in her normal travel regalia, minus her lute, backpack, and weapons, as she gave them up before entering the throne room. Deeya knew much more than she wanted to know about the Kell dynasty. They were mostly good folk, a monarchy that cared about their people. But there were bad eggs in every batch.... Sometimes the bad eggs got to sit upon the throne, sometimes they got the even more powerful position of whispering into the ear of the person that sat upon the throne.... Either way, Deeya knew this was a trap.

"The honorable El'Mindeeya Do'Katal. The Emerald Bard."

The herald was off to the side, he announced her, and then exited a hidden side door. Deeya scanned the balcony above the throne room, so many dark corners.... Deeya's elven eyes saw no one though, she was alone with the two Kells. Alarm bells were ringing in her head, but she ignored them. She was far more prepared for this trap than she let on, if it was indeed a trap. It felt like one, but Deeya did not know why they would try to capture her, she had just saved the realm from being subverted by a magically controlled Duke....

"Hail and well met, Elf Bard."

Deeya bowed respectfully to the King. She was always respectful when in other people's countries. "Hail and well met to thee, your Majesty."

Prince Kell stepped forward and explained, in detail, what had transpired in Duke Quinlan's castle. The King responded with, "Disgraceful! How could that happen under our very noses? How did you manage to slay the evil woman, Bard?"

Deeya shrugged, "I got lucky, maybe she didn't expect me to have a weapon."

The Prince nodded, "Yes, a bow, from what I understand."

The King leaned forward, "So you did not...use some form of Elfish magic?"

Deeya gave an incredulous look. "Magic? I might be an Elf, your majesty, but I was not raised by elves. I never learned how to use their magic, if they possess such a thing." In all honesty they did to some degree. All elves have a connection to the life that grows around them. They can feed off of it, manipulating it in different ways. But, honestly again, Deeya had barely learned how to talk to trees, channeling the life force of the world was something she figured she would never master.

The Prince frowned and said, "So all the destruction in the chamber was caused by her alone? How did you escape as unharmed as you were?"

Deeya shrugged. "I'm fast on my feet, mainly."

The King stayed leaning forward, scrutinizing the bard with degrading eyes, "So, you cannot use magic at all?"

Deeya shrugged again and said, "Nope, I only know the magic of music."

The King leaned back, giving Deeya a disgusted look, as his voice boomed, "We shall see."

Deeya frowned. She opened her mouth to ask, "What do you mean by that?" but nothing came out. In fact, now that she tried, she found that there was no air for her to breathe. She instinctively looked up and saw a human in a dark hood standing on the balcony. How had she missed that wizard? He was chanting, holding out his hand. Deeya could see his mouth moving, could see the force he was putting into his words, yet everything was dead silent. She thought fast, trying to understand that there was a bubble of no air all around her head. During all of this, she saw a shadow move and ducked. Barely avoiding Prince Condar Kell's blade.

Deeya pivoted and lashed out in defense, punching the man in the kidneys with her left fist, his ribs with her right fist (at least one rib she could feel break under her punch), and then started her spin to kick the stunned man in the face. Mid turn though, Deeya felt a stabbing pain in her thigh.

The pain caused her to falter in her kick. She grasped for the arrow embedded in her leg as the spin she was in twisted her around till she fell to her other knee. She spent what seemed like an eternity on that knee. For the first time in a very long time, Deeya was completely powerless. She had given up her weapons upon entry, and, she realized very quickly, as she tried to inhale, that without air, she could not breathe in to sing.

Her quick movements had already used up some of the air reserve within her...more like quite a bit. Spots started forming in her vision as she looked at the floor. She was dazed, but when a second arrow cut her hand, narrowly missing her leg again, she snapped back to reality. Her grim reality.

She stood up to attempt to defend herself. She tried to turn to see where the arrows were coming from, but all she saw was the third arrow rushing towards her. She moved as quickly as she could, but she still deftly caught the arrow in her left shoulder. The impact was immense, throwing her backwards.

She flew until she felt her back hit one of the many pillars of the great hall. The pillar had kept her from falling. Oddly, though, she found she could not move forward either. She looked down at the arrow, and realized only a few inches of it were coming out of her shoulder before the feathers. The arrow had pinned her to the pillar behind her. Deeya clutched the arrow, trying to break it, but was unable as her strength was fading from lack of air.

She turned her green eyes to the King. He sat back down on his throne with a huge grin on his face, his blue eyes glinting in the weak torchlight of the room, as he laid his bow across his lap. Deeya struggled a moment more, her mind racing to find inspiration on what she could do, then, finally, she went limp, and hung from the arrow like a drape.

The King smiled at his nephew who waved for the wizard to come down. "I suppose you have a plan on how to remove that thing from my throne room?"

The Prince nodded with a wince, as he held his side. He could feel the bruise swelling around the broken rib. "That I do, Uncle Edward." He turned towards the limp bard, Deeya, with disgust in his eyes as he picked up his sword that he had dropped when she had hit him. "She, or her kin, will not meddle in our plots again."

The King laughed heartily. "No, *it* won't," he said, emphasizing the "it" when it came to the elf. "Shame it killed Ryn'Vey, that one might have been an elf, but at least it was one of the tamable ones. We'll never find a mage as powerful as that again."

The Prince smirked as he jerked the arrow out of Deeya's shoulder and she crumpled to the ground in a heap. "Ryn'Vey had a daughter, my liege. After I bury this one, I will seek out Ashengrey A'Taril and turn her to our cause."

The King smiled greedily. The wizard came out of the same door that the herald had exited earlier. He walked up beside the prince, knelt beside the body of the bard, pushed his hood back to reveal an older man with chiseled features. He held a bare hand to the Emerald Bard's lifeless body, chanted a few syllables and concentrated on the results. "She be dead, Your Grace, as you requested."

Prince Condar knelt beside the corpse of his nemesis, the Emerald Bard and whispered in her ear, "I finally have revenge for what you did to my father and me."

The King waved his hand, "Remove that *thing*, Nephew," he said, referring to Deeya's corpse.

The Prince stood and smiled. "At once my liege, I know the perfect spot for her."

—

Condar always thought that elves were lighter
than they looked, like they were some magical being that
had less weight than they actually did. He had often
heard the stories about them walking on top of snow.
But no, the body was limp, heavy, and hard to move, as
were most cadavers. As much as the Prince hated
exertion, he was a prince after all..., he knew he had to
help Amalric to finish before the dawn. Every time the
shovel dug into the dirt, though, he knew the exact
reason he worked alongside the mage: No witnesses to
what they had done. The Emerald Bard was to just
vanish from the world.

Only the three of them knew anything. The mage
was the herald, who was the guard who took the bard's
gear. The king was an idiot who would never fully
understand why he did what he did. He was driven by a
deep xenophobia toward elves, something Condar
himself had instilled in his weak minded uncle. The
emotion had deepened after the death of Edward's father,
Condar's grandfather, King Leland, who had been killed
as a direct result of El'Mindeeya's elven ineptitude.

The Kell dynasty had a rather normal line of
succession. When Leland was killed by a dragon, the
line passed to his first son, Trank. Trank, though, only
lasted on the throne for a year. He was deposed by the
public due to the fact that he had conspired to have the
mission to kill the aforementioned dragon go wrong so
that he could ascend the throne. Since Trank was
deposed, his only son, Condar, did not follow him to the
throne, instead it fell to Trank's siblings. Leland had
three children, Trank was the first, then there was a

middle daughter, and a younger son. It came out that the coup was helped along by the middle daughter, so Edward, the youngest son inherited the throne.

Condar tossed the last of the earth aside, the last he was going to dig, at least, as rain started falling from the sky. A shallow grave for the elf that had cost him everything, as the coup that removed his father from the throne, had been helped along, not only by his aunt, but by this dead elf.

He turned to look at the body of the bard as the rain made her elven skin glint in the light from the moon which peeked out from behind the storm clouds from time to time. The bard might have taken away his eventual legitimate ascension to the throne, but she gave him something that could be considered better. Edward was the perfect man for the throne as he was a dimwitted buffoon who could not rule without someone whispering into his ear. Condar, Edward's own nephew, was Edward's lead advisor. Condar ruled the kingdom, yet took none of the blame for the things that went wrong. He could never have ruled so freely if he wore the crown himself, he was a self-styled puppet master.

He climbed out of the just over knee deep hole and grabbed the bard's arm and started dragging her towards her final resting place. The mage, Amalric pulled the bard's leg. The bard unceremoniously flopped into the hole like an old rag doll, splashing into the wet mud at the bottom. The dirt melted into mud as the pair slung it onto the bard, each sling of the shovel resulted in a sickening "splut." Finally, though, they were finished.

Fittingly, he picked up his father's sword, the sword that was taken from King Trank when he was deposed from power. He jabbed it into the ground like a head stone and Amalric hung the crude sign around the hilt. Together, they walked back towards the castle as lightning flashed all around them and rain soaked the world. Condar had to get ready for his journey before the sun arose, as he had a long way to go during the day. Such a very long way...especially in the storm that was coming.

--

In the meadow there stood an old rusty sword stabbed into the ground. The night was dark and flushed with rain, which had been falling for almost an entire day's time, which was coming down in a torrent. Lightning flashed all around, illuminating the mound of freshly moved earth as rivulets of water streaked its surface. On the grave marker of a sword hung a sign noting the occasion of the funeral with these hastily painted words:

"Here lies a true bard
Who lied all her days.
Here we did discard
All her ignorant green clichés."

The sword stood like a headstone for the mound of earth that moved slightly.... Without warning, a part of the mound pushed skyward, and a hand emerged from the wet ground, streams of mud sluicing down the arm like the afterbirth of some grim rebirth. Like the dead come back to life, the muddy female birthed herself from the grave, gulping air. She was barely recognizable as an elf, her clothes torn and clinging to her, were caked with filth and her own blood. Her face, streaked with the grime from her grave, turned slowly to take in her surroundings as she shivered violently. Finally, her stark green eyes focused on the sword and then the sign. She staggered forward, her ruined boots sinking into the muck of the mound she was once buried in, and picked up the sign. After she read the words, hatred spread over her face and, with a dagger, she scratched in a new poem over the words that were painted on:

"From hence came the Emerald Bard
Clawing her way out of the grave
Her enemies better be on their guard
For everyone should fear Music's true rage."

She hung the sign back around the hilt of the old, rusted blade and tried to stand. It was a struggle at first, almost as if she was a newborn trying to find her footing for the first time. Finally, her body rose away from the ground and she turned her mud stained face upwards, into the rain. She stood as erect as she could, triumphantly arching her back as she stretched the aches of having been technically dead for, what she hoped was, one full cycle of day. Mud streamed down the curves of her body, proving that the entity that birthed from the grave was indeed a female, and her clumped short hair fell away revealing her elven ears.

If anyone would have witness the scene, as it was lit with flashes of lightning, they would have heard a soft sort of humming. About the same time, they would have realized that the humming was coming from the mud caked female, and they would have witnessed a strange bubble appear around her. A bubble that, at first pushed then, diverted the rain around her in a perfect sphere.

In the flashing light of the midnight storm, she examined herself, taking note of the ruined, mud stained, shredded clothing. She also checked the wounds that put her in the ground. All healed. For just a brief moment more, she thought about the spell that allowed her to live.

She had only glanced upon it within the book that Tessa had given her, she had never had time to test it out. Some bards called it Feign Death, others had called it Stasis. Either way, it put your body into a death state for up to a full day. During that time, the body healed. Most importantly though, those under the spell needed no air and took on the appearance of death.

The mud soak figure remembered being Deeya, remembered fading into unconsciousness from lack of air and pain, and remembered the idea to cast that spell. It was cast by simple tongue clicks, and even though there was no air around her, she had been able to close her mouth, fill it with exhaled air, and hear the tongue clicks within her own head.

With the memories of life, came the memories of the pain of dying. With the pain of dying came the revelation that on this night, there was no Emerald Bard, for she had been buried. In her stead stood a disheveled, mud and blood soaked female form that steeled herself for the vengeance to come.

Again, if someone would have been there to witness this event at all, they would have been shocked when the female elf, with her shredded, wet clothing clinging to her every curve, started humming a second tune. They would have heard the second tune interweave with the first, becoming two distinct melodies battling each other for dominance. They were not being hummed at the same time, but alternated in a magical, lyrical way. The bubble around her seemed to pulsate with life, trying to collapse only to be brought back to life when the tune changed back to the tune that brought it into existence.

The pulsing of the bubble seemed to resonate like it had its own heartbeat. Then, without warning, the female elf became a streak, running from the scene at a pace that was beyond human, outpacing the fastest horse that had ever existed.

And with her leaving, the rain fell again upon the mound and the sword stood like a warning to the storm: vengeance had awoken and was now falling upon this land.

--

The guards to the castle were anything but inept. They guarded the gate in the dark of the night. They both wanted to talk about Prince Kell the night before, walking by with that mysterious wizard friend of his, carrying a large bag. But they knew better than to do such a thing. Their duty was to remain vigilant, to guard the castle gate that was left open at night in case any of the country folk needed refuge.

The Kells had always governed the land as such. No matter how much the current monarch hated the

people, the people were the life source of the realm.
Their protection was paramount.

The two guards were glad they stood under the
eaves of the wall, it kept them out of the rain, which was
coming down like a river.

"'ave ya ever seen such a monsoon?"

The other shook his head, "Never."

"Ominous, is it not?"

The one man looked to the other who had spoken
first and gave him a queer look under his visor. He
personally disliked the man and his superstitions. But it
actually was raining quite hard. At this rate, the moat
might overflow. It happened rarely, but it was such a
concern that the road had been raised just in case many
years ago. He sighed to himself and started to look away
from his superstitious partner when lightning flashed.

Out of the corner of his eye, he swore he saw a
drenched, dead looking boy out on the road. Judging by
the statues' height at the end of the drawbridge's landing,
the boy was about 5 feet tall with short, dark hair. But it
was just a flash. He squinted and watched that particular
spot for several breaths, waiting to see it again.

Lightning finally arced again, though it did so
entirely too close for comfort. The sound and the
brightness happening almost at the same time. He did
not see the boy again, but he swore he saw some form of
heat shimmer coming from the drawbridge a few feet
away from his post. The clap had happened so close it
had caused his ears to ring.

The superstitious guard cursed, having been scared
by the sudden peal of thunder being so close. "Fuck my
head off!" He held a hand to his armored chest, wanting

to see if his heart was beating hard enough to feel it, as it was pounding in his ears. Alas, he couldn't feel his chest because of the breastplate he wore. "Could there be a worse night to wear steel armor?"

The other man kept his eyes forward, wanting to make sure that he was not seeing things. He replied though, in a cautious tone, "Aye, that might very well be true, but at least it doesn't soak through like leather."

The ringing in the guards' ears was loud, but even if their ears had not been deafened by the clap of thunder, they still would not have heard the soft music being sung that drifted directly between them. The song was an amazing song, laced with more of the same magic that started at the burial mound in the meadow. The melody made all who heard it unable to see or hear what the singer did not want them to perceive.

A few moments later the one guard pointed towards the stone pathway between them and said, "Hey, where did that mud come from?"

They both looked down at the puddle that had formed on the stones between them. It abruptly ended in the courtyard behind them, which was its own big pit of mud at this point. The superstitious guard gave a shrug. They both knew that no one could have walked between them, unnoticed, leaving a puddle of mud.... Must have been the wind....

--

Once she had passed the overly muddy courtyard, the dark figure entered the castle proper. There were guards on patrol all around, but they were all easily bypassed with songs that kept the female figure hidden from view. The main hallway of the castle was completely empty, the only guards positioned at the entrance. There were several small rooms to the side of the hallway, each fulfilling different purposes. One room was specifically to house wet coats, cloaks, and other items that were not needed under the roof of the castle.

The inside of the coat room was, at times, brightly lit by the lightning arcing all around the region. There was a drain in the floor of the closet, to drain away any moisture that were to roll off wet coats. Mud leading up to this room was a given, but away...had to be avoided.

A quick burst of sound inside the coatroom, perfectly timed to a thunderclap, left the late night visitor dry, though still horrendously disheveled. Her hair was a complete mess, though that was one of the reasons she always kept it short, so she never had to do anything with it, and her green clothes were ripped to shreds, though at this point she was not too concerned with modesty. It was hard to call what was left of her clothes green any longer, as they were stained brown and red all over.

The disheveled female elf silently left the coat closet and made her way through the castle. As mentioned before, she had been in this castle in a former life, and she knew it well. She knew exactly what she was looking for. There was a store room, just off the servant's section, where all the trash was collected before getting carted away or burned. And that is where she found it all, well...almost all.

The Emerald Bard's pack rested off to the side, with all the weapons tied to it. The female elf who crawled out of the Emerald Bard's grave searched for a moment, but could not find the lute, or its waterproof slip case. She finally went back to the pack and opened it up. She pulled out a few changes of green clothes and stacked them neatly to the side. In the very bottom of the pack, she opened a hidden inside pouch and pulled out a solid black suit.

She peeled away the ruined clothes without hesitation. She did one final check across her nude body to make sure all the wounds healed thoroughly, all the while ignoring the unique sound her bare feet were making as they echoed off the close walls of the interior. After becoming fully satisfied that she was in perfect condition, she held her breasts and tightly wrapped them and her ribs with a thick cloth that would keep them in place and out of the way for the combat she knew was coming. Finally, she donned the suit. It fit snugly to her body, with hidden leather padding sewn into it. The outfit had been designed for one purpose and one purpose only, dexterous, murderous movement.

She quickly laced up the calf high black leather boots that had thick, yet soft, leather tread on their bottoms. She then put on her belt. The belt was bulky, but it was the belt she always wore, even though this outfit hid any embellishment that might shine or have an insignia on it. She finally stood, strapped on the weapons, and the pack, wrapped the black mask around her face, and pulled up the black hood.

She had no name when she wore this suit, no title. But she always had one mission. Revenge had come to the castle that held the seat of power in this country. The castle where King Kell slept, not knowing he was awaiting a visitor before morning's light broke upon the horizon.

—

King Edward Kell was normally a deep sleeper. It was still dark in the room, the sun's morning light was only just starting to form a line across the horizon. It was far too early to be up. It had been a dream that had awakened him. The same dream that had woken him many a night before. The one where he was surrounded by spies. His nephew Condar fell to an assassin's blade, his only trusted ally in all of this, that odd mage friend of Condar was nowhere to be found. Besides the terror, the King always wondered why he trusted that mage so well, he did not even know the man's name....

His sheets were soaked with sweat, but it was his sweat, not the sweat of his concubine that had left after he was done with her. The cold sweat gave more of a chill to the night air, especially without that damnable whore there to keep him warm. He would have to punish the woman for her insolence.

Shadows, though, moved, reminding him of the terror of the dream. The shock of the assassins killing his nephew, how they surrounded the King, how terrified he was. In fact, one of the shadows in the room looked like one of the assassins from his dream. Clad in black, looking like a shadow with stark, steely light eyes.

Then he heard the whispers. Soft at first. It was a song, of some kind. He was still groggy, unbalanced, not thinking straight. Why would a song scare him? Why would a song remind him of his dream, remind him of cowering before the blade, and remind him of the question they were asking him before they were to kill him?

"What were your plans?"

The fat man blathered before the shadow at the end of the bed, revealing it all. "My ancestors have ruled this land with too lax a hand. All our neighbors are armed to the teeth, and are watching us like we are ripe for the picking...but little do they know.... I've been raising an army to take the weakest kingdom around us, as soon as my spies return, and tell me which that is, I'll be ready to strike."

The King glanced around quickly, trying to see when other shadows in the room where going to move towards the bed and deliver the killing stab. In his not quite awake mind, they all seemed to be ready to pounce, every shadow in the room, except for the one at the foot of the bed, which stood there, still as a statue. The words from the assassin came clearer now, without the melodic music that was lulling him into needing to tell everything. The words were cold, stark, and undeniable.

"Why kill the bard?"

The King wet his lips and shivered. "Condar said she was a spy. That she had uncovered how we tried to control Duke Quinlan. How we were using the sorceress to create an army though some kind of magical coercion."

"So Condar was the one who came up with the idea to use magic to twist the minds of innocent people to make you an army?"

The King shook his head. "No, 'twas my idea, but only Condar had the means. That foul woman that mage of his knew, Ryn'Vey." The eyes of the shadow at the foot of the bed seemed to narrow. The King swallowed nervously and continued on. "She came to us, hearing of what we wanted, and offered us everything we wanted.. .if...."

"If what?"

The glare from the shadow was unbearable. The King was shivering, though not from the chill of the air. "If we broke her daughter."

It was then that the shadow finally moved. It moved with the fluid grace of an assassin ready to pounce. It walked around the bed like a cat stalking its prey. Suddenly, the whispering song seemed to get louder in his brain as the shadow got closer. Just because the King failed to notice it, does not mean it ever stopped.... He was terrified, he wanted to curl up and hide under the covers, so none of the shadows could see him, especially the one that was stalking him. But he could not move. Instead, he stared at the shadow's face, staying transfixed on the shadowy assassin that he knew had come to kill him.

But then something odd happened. Something that grounded the room around him outside of a dream. The shadow simply walked in front of the window. It was a solid person, a real person, not a shadow from his dream.

The King narrowed his eyes and said, "Wait.... Who are you?"

The shadow stopped and seemed to sigh. The spell of the music was broken over something so simple. A shadow casting its own shadow. There was nothing else to do but to finish what was started.

"King Edward Kell, I am the ghost of the Bard you buried." The shadowy assassin reached up and pulled down the black fabric in front of her face as she spoke. The King's eyes widened tremendously. "I still feel the pain of your arrow in my shoulder, even this far into death."

The King stammered, "So...so it's true? You were a supernatural spy conjured by the necromancers from the Aldantan Kingdom to the west?"

"No, I'm just an elf, from the Forested Isle. If I even had been a spy, then I was a spy for an immortal people far from here, on an Island inside the Great Inner Sea." The light from the rising sun, even though it had not crested the horizon, shown just bright enough for the shadow's green eyes to glint behind her facial expression of grim determination. "Where is Condar Kell?"

The King shook his head. "No, he will be next in line to the throne when you kill me, I will not divulge that information." His eyes widened again, showing his words to be a bluff as he tried to hide behind the covers. But then his eyes got wider as an elven sword appeared in the shadow's hand.

"I'll give you one more chance to answer. I already know he is not within the castle. He left early yesterday morning, but where is he going?"

The King locked his eyes with those undead green eyes from the shadow. He nodded. "Isn't it obvious? He's going back to finish what we started. That filth you killed had a daughter. He is going to find her, break her, and finish raising the army before it's too late. Just..
.leave him alone. If he dies, then the Kingdom falls into

the hands of my sister's son, who's too young...so my incompetent sister will rule in his stead...."

The shadow seemed to smile, "Yes...she will. And she will return this kingdom to a state where the monarchy is loved by the people, unlike what you have garnered in your reign, which has been far too long."

The King shook his head, then lunged off the bed, screaming, "No! Guards! Help me!"

The shadow shook its head, as it watched the portly king flail around like a beached seal on the floor.

"They cannot hear you, fool. Only I can...."

The King continued to flail around, in his sickly, almost comedic fashion. It he had not been so obese and nude, the shadow might have not been able to continue on with a straight face. But it did.

"I pronounce sentence over you in the name of your people. The same people that you had flogged for speaking out against your policies, the same people that you had imprisoned for rallying to your sister when your brother showed his true colors, the same people you had put to death for loving your father, the same people you were coercing into your army by the use of foul magics."

The King was almost hysterical. He was trying to get up and run, to get to a sword by the door. The instant he gained his footing and started to rise from the ground, a hum buzzed in his ears, his feet suddenly left the floor, and he was forcibly thrown against the wall, where he found himself being held by an unseen force as his feet dangled some distance above the solid floor beneath him. The shadow casually walked towards him as he hung there, held by some invisible magic.

The shadow stopped its stride in front of him and looked up into his eyes as they drained of the will to struggle any longer. The King's eyes stared out of the window, looking towards the last sunrise he would ever see. The sun broke upon the horizon in the most brilliant explosion of light. It was beautiful and awe-inspiring.

The shadow spoke softly, deadly, "I pronounce your sentence to be death."

The King wept tears at that point. Of knowing he did wrong, and of the beautiful sunrise. He whispered, "May the Kell dynasty rule forever, With an open hand, Love for the people it governs, and show Mercy to all who live."

The Kell family motto, first spoke by its original patriarch as he passed away quietly in his bed. The elven blade cut through the air with the slightest of whispers as the assassin added one last thought:

"Through your Sister's son."

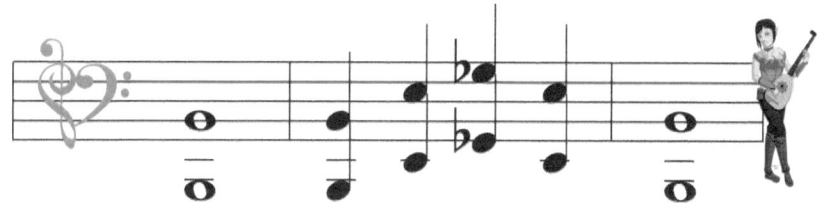

Movement 2: A Simple Matter of Escaping

The head bounced once after it hit the floor and
rolled away. The dark figure stepped back and let the
headless body collapse onto the floor as blood started
collecting into a quickly growing puddle that was slowly
oozing towards her. The shadow looked upon the scene
and pushed back her hood, revealing her short messy
mop of hair. She allowed a single tear to escape, but she
wiped it off before it got very far. She then allowed her
anger to wash over her once more, allowed the fact that
all this had been set in motion by one man:

Condar Kell.

Her death, his own failed ascent to the throne
which had put Edward there, and all the punishments
and pain that had been dealt to every peasant in the
realm. Her face took on a mask of rigid resolve again,
murderous intent. She replaced the black cloth that hid
her face, pulled up the hood, and got back to work.

Some would shed tears for the slain monarch, but
others would rejoice. Every family has bad apples

hanging from the branches, and all it takes is one bad apple to spoil the bushel. The shadow turned and walked towards the window. She might tell herself that this is culling bad apples, but what she really thought about was how the King had smiled while watching as Deeya's life slowly ebbed from her from the arrows that he had shot into her flesh. That smile burned into her memory as the feeling of helplessness blossomed as she struggled for breath. He had smiled in joyful triumph at the death of her, an elf. There should never be anyone in power who does not respect the life of other sentient beings.

A murder for a murderer.

The problem now was that the castle was alive with activity. The songs only worked on all those that heard it. There was no sneaking out the way the shadow had snuck in. No, there was only one way out now.

--

Gerald enjoyed his job. He had been a member of the King's guard all his life and, although he was not the most senior of the guards, he was able to select his time on guard duty. The graveyard shift. No one ever bothered the King at night. All you had to do, was stand here by the door, and make sure no one came in or out. Unless, of course it was one of the beauties the King kept in his harem. Seeing their naked perfection walk by in the middle of the night made it far easier to plow his ugly, fat wife when he got home.

Being the bedroom guard also kept one out of danger, out of the public, and the graveyard shift had extra pay since you had to stay up all night to do it. And the best perk? You didn't even have to see the King at all. He went into his bedroom on someone else's shift, and the shift changed when the new guard walked up with the servant bringing breakfast.

Speaking of the servant bringing breakfast....

Gerald had no idea what her name was, but he liked to call her Rose. She was more beautiful than any of the women in the King's harem. Her dress plunged deeply, showing off an amount of cleavage that Gerald imagined he was coming home to when he was really coming home to his wife. As many women as he had seen naked come to and from the King's door, he craved to see this one woman naked.

This morning, as with most mornings, he turned a blind eye to her bleary eyes. Yet he was grateful for those bleary, tired eyes, because they completely missed him ogling her impressively displayed chest. This was the only King he had ever served that liked his servants to dress in such a provocative way. Gerald might have enjoyed it, but he still found it degrading when he thought about the portly fat king ogling this amazingly curvy beauty of a woman that he could never truly appreciate or please. No matter how detestable it was, a King is a King, and Gerald knew to keep his mouth shut. Besides, behind the beautiful busty maid was his replacement, Rikard. It was time to go home and wake his wife so he could make the ugly wench worship his manhood.

Gerald opened the door for the servant, trying not to ogle her cleavage up close, he was a married man after all, and being caught ogling was...well...tacky. He then started the silly ceremony for changing the guards with Rikard. Luckily it was a quick ceremony.

Halfway through the silly dance, as he liked to call it, the inevitable scream halted them trying not to be embarrassed. Both men looked at each other, drew their swords and stepped into the room.

Gerald tried to make sense of the room in a glance. Headless body, head, puddle of blood, screaming young woman, and someone dressed in all black jumping out the window. Rikard was young, too young to have fought in a war, thusly, he had never seen a dead body before. But Gerald was not distracted. He instantly ran to stop the assassin, but he did not get there in time.

The lithe person in black leapt out the window with grace, Gerald watched the person spin in the air. He then watched as the rope he had not noticed got tight and the figure swung back towards the wall below him. He gripped the rope in front of him, but it was too late, the assassin vanished in a shower of glass as the figure had swung through a window in the room below. Gerald turned, ran, and started yelling.

"Assassin! Rally the guard! Assassin!"

His mind raced as he ran to the stairs.

What was the assassin's plan?

The best way to catch a criminal was to think like a criminal. Going further into the castle was suicide, so going down the stairs of the King's Tower was crazy, especially with the castle on alarm now. He got to the door of the level below the King's chambers and before he could open it, it exploded, sending shards of wood at him. Pieces stuck into the gaps of his armor, causing intense pain, but it was nothing substantial.

The pain was forgotten as the assassin came through the hole where the door had been, flying directly at him as the pieces of jagged wood bounced off the wall behind him and fell to the floor. The assassin had two weapons and was insanely fast. He blocked a sword strike as he unsheathed his blade and parried an axe blow as he quickly pirouetted, putting himself between the assassin and the route that led to the stairs downwards. But to his surprise, the assassin quickly turned, without any hesitation, and ran up the stairs, back towards the King's Chamber.

Gerald chased after, his yells of warning, "Assassin! Rally the guard!" continued to bounce off the walls, which finally seemed to have gotten someone's attention. He could hear armored men and women running up the stairs from below. Above the cacophony below, though, he heard the sounds of the fight which had started above him. He found himself climbing the stairs faster than he ever thought possible as he raced to help Rikard, who was in an amazing duel with the assassin. Rikard might have gotten the job of King's Guard because of having a powerful, influential father, but he was an absolute artist with his thin blade. The blade often found him as the butt of many a joke in the guardsman's barracks, as it was thin and almost dainty. But damned if the man did not know how to wield it.....

The assassin and Rikard danced with their weapons, it was like watching poetry in motion. Both combatants were masters with their respective weapons. The assassin wielded their sword and axe with a skill that was going to overtake Rikard within moments. Gerald's mind raced as he tried to figure out how he could join the assault. Then, to Gerald's amazement, he saw Rikard score a slight hit on the inside of the assassin's guard, cutting the assassin's shoulder.

As soon as the blow landed though, Gerald's veteran eyes could see that the black clad assassin allowed Rikard's strike to hit. The wound itself was taken to gain advantage. The assassin used its unhurt shoulder to ram into Rikard's exposed chest. The assassin used the momentum to trip Rikard on the stairs, roll off of him, and leap up the stairs like a child playing a game. Rikard cursed as he struggled to get back up on the incline of the stairs where he fell, his thick armor hindering him more than it helped.

Gerald, who chased after the assassin by running past Rikard, soon heard him from behind running up the stairs as both guardsmen chased after the assassin.

The King's chambers were at the last landing before the top of the tower. It had always been a struggle for the recently slain king to maneuver up and down the stairs daily, considering his weight, but the views were the best in the castle that most other kings had fully enjoyed. One single flight up led to the trap door to the roof, which slammed shut in Gerald's face as he got to it. He cursed and slammed his armored shoulder into the wooden trap door, the same instant he heard the bar to lock it slam into place.

Rikard ran up behind Gerald screaming. The old veteran knew what was going to happen, but he still stepped out of the rookie's way. Rikard slammed into the trap door with as much might, if not more, as Gerald had done, with the same result.

Rikard looked at the solid wooden trap door, nursing the armored shoulder that was now dented, scuffed, with sore flesh underneath, and said, "Why did he go up there?"

Gerald's gruff, veteran voice muttered, "Maybe the little shit can fly."

--

The black clad assassin turned from the door and pulled the backpack from her injured shoulder. The song had already closed the wound, but it still ached below the healed skin. The sun was getting higher than the assassin wanted it to, as the last vestiges that were the shadows of night across the world below were shrinking back towards the horizon, and she needed to be down there to vanish amongst them. The shadowy figure fiddled fiercely with her backpack, opening hidden folds and turning it into some form of contraption, as a new, vigorous loud pounding started from the trap door behind her.

--

Gerald was in front, aiming the battering ram at the door above him, pulling it upwards into the thick wood. This was hard work, because of the angle of the stairs and the angle of the door. But his fellow guardsmen knew what they were doing.

Once they got a nick in the door, where the ram could gain traction, the door started splintering away. Shards of wood rained down upon the guardsmen, who had to turn their heads to keep from getting wood in their eyes. The pounding was intense, the sound reverberating off the walls of the stairwell in a deafening way, but soon enough the door gave way, splintering outwards in a loud crack.

Gerald haphazardly dropped his part of the battering ram, shoved his way up through the splinters of the door and was the first on the roof. He scanned the scene, looking for any sign of the insane interloper.

The rising sun, to the East, was a blinding light, but against that blinding light, he saw movement. A movement that suddenly vanished.

He ran to the edge and looked down, his eyes barely discerning a triangular shadow against the background of the lake far below.

The guard captain, a tall man with long blond hair in a messy braid said, "Where is the assassin?"

Gerald pointed, "Some form of flying contraption."

The captain squinted, watching the black triangle bank slightly in the air, as it briefly caught the light one last time before it passed back into the shadow of horizon against the predawn light. He cursed and walked away, giving orders and shouting for some semblance of order as the entire regiment of guardsmen spilled out of the trap door onto the roof of the tower.

Gerald sighed deeply, realizing that he was in for a very long day. The chaos that was about to ensue might destroy the kingdom. He sighed and rubbed his eyes, as it had already been a long night.

As he blinked away the spots in his eyes, he looked to a shadowy section of the raised parapet. He took a few steps towards a particular crenelation and knelt down to read the words scribbled in a stark white chalk:

"Long Live King Gundar Kell."

Gerald blinked. Gundar was in line *after* Condar. He turned and ran to the guard captain, "Sir! The assassin, he's going after Prince Condar."

The captain turned and looked at Gerald, then at the chalk that Gerald was pointing towards. He rubbed his grizzled chin in thought, turned towards his men and started barking orders. The fastest four horses were to be taken by guardsmen to find and warn the new King as other guard contingents were to find the deceased King Edward's sister and her son, to insure that Gundar was protected, as well. As much as Gerald knew that this was indeed a dark day for the kingdom of Kell, he knew how the former King's reign had been and how Prince Condar's hand had influenced all the bad.... Gundar had a chance to be a good king.... He shoved the treasonous thoughts aside and volunteered to guard Gundar personally...how could he sleep anyways?

--

There was an unbelievable joy in gliding through the air, strapped to light cloth wings. The air circulated around the dark shadow of the assassin, rustling her short hair under the hood that was threatening to get blown back. The metal that made up the triangular frame was lightweight, alien material, the same that made up her bow. The cloth material of the glider was a lightweight material that, unfortunately, was extremely fragile. The light weight of it all made for easy storage in the confines of hidden pockets of her backpack, but the fragility of it made the glider an emergency only risk. As the bard, she had only used it a handful of times, and each time was as thrilling as the first.

But she knew she could not get caught up in the thrill of the moment. Every time she had used the glider prior was the same story: there was always a next part to the plan. Part of her had always hated the double life. The shadow was the bard's other side, the deadly, skilled spy who did what she needed to do. She was indeed a spy for the elves, as Condar had feared, but she was normally just an information relay, someone who just collected information about the world and brought it home to her Monarch. Even though she was capable of clandestine operations, she refused to do them. No, the bard only donned the black outfit when the occasion absolutely called for it.

This mess that she found herself in, Condar would claim, was her own doing. The treetops whizzed by below her chest as she thought upon the near comedy of errors that had transpired just over two decades earlier, on her quest for the Goddess of Music. The quest had led her here, to the Kells. Condar had one side of the story, the black clad shadowy assassin held the other, and soon it would all be resolved. The escape was the easy part of the overall plan. There were very few parts left, the most important, though, involved more bloodshed. The next part of the plan, required her to find Condar before he knew she was coming. She knew she was in a race against time.

--

Prince Condar rode his horse lazily after the long, hard ride of the day. The sun was beginning to set in the distance and for once there was not an inn for some ways.

He was avoiding inns on purpose, though.

The guards with him wore armor that clanked loudly, and Condar Kell was getting extremely tired of the noise. Luckily the scout had returned back with news of a good place to set up a tent in a field.

The prince ran his fingers through his red beard, thinking about how events had gone against him recently. It had been a hard two days ride, and only then did he realize that his beard needed trimming. Between the bard interfering in the politics of the land, as she had done so long ago, and his uncle's, King Edward's, obsession with the kingdom of Aldantan, he had forgotten his own personal grooming.

All this reverie about problems that were keeping him from noticing things like his own beard, kept him from noticing the black figure perched in a nearby tree. It was just a shadow, though, and easily dismissed.

The scouts had ridden ahead with the cart toting the tent so they could set it up without Condar having to wait. The Prince had become so used to his guard being efficient he did not give a single thought the fact that the tent was setup by the time he rode up to it.

The entire campsite, itself, was not far from being completed. Condar had never rode to war, never seen how regimented men with dogged determination worked, never seen a war campsite. There was no reference for him to appreciate how truly well trained and disciplined his small contingent of guards really were. Instead, without a single glance at them, no acknowledgment at all, he handed over the reins of his horse and entered his tent.

The figure in black had come a very long way this day, and had gotten lucky running across Condar on the main road. The prince was not making any effort to hide himself, and why should he? He buried the evidence of the murder himself and all he was doing was riding to his dismantled army to rebuild it.

A mission that would involve capturing Ashengrey.

The black clad figure knew that was not going to happen, Ash was long gone by now. But the thought of him actually capturing Ash, knowing the thought processes of men like him, knowing what he was imagining he could do to the stunning blonde beauty....

The shadow stayed perched and watched the scene for a good while, waiting for an opportunity. Until finally one arrived. But there was worry in the shadow's heart, as there was no sign of the mage that had caused her death by removing the air that she breathed before she had died....

--

Inside the tent, Condar was going over the next day's ride with the captain of his guard. She was a tall, muscular, well-endowed woman, who showed off her endowment with her specially made armor. Her specially forged armor was designed for sex appeal, not defense. A deliberate distraction, crafted for men like

Condar to ogle and underestimate. The captain of the guard knew what Condar really needed most of all by his side, closest of all his guardsmen....

"We will get to Duke Quinlan's castle just after midday, your majesty."

Condar nodded. "Good, I'm getting tired of the constant clanking of armor."

The woman nodded, "As am I, but we have the best men in the realm, they will be able to train the troops you plan to make. Hard men, vicious, who don't mind whipping others into submission."

Condar nodded while moving an ancient lute out of his chair before sitting down in it. "We were so close before...."

The guard nodded, "True, but this woman will bend easily enough to our will. Just as I did, under your charms."

Condar looked haggard and tired. He looked into the woman's eyes, without the lust he normally used to look at her. "Will she? Her mother, or sister, or whatever the hell those two were to each other...she had made it pretty clear that it was an impossibility with her."

The guard took off her helmet, letting her long black hair flow out of the metal encasement. Condar could not help but notice how attractive she was when she did such a thing. She strode around the table, like a panther stalking her prey. As she dropped her helmet upon the floor next to the lute, she said, "Oh, I know a few tricks that might work on her."

He put his hand on her armored midriff, feeling the faux muscles that had been forged into the steel. He smiled into her pretty face and said, "You know all the best tricks, my oldest friend."

With that, she kissed him, with the passion of an old lover with a craving for so very much more. He slid his hand up to the woman's armored breasts. She moaned into the kiss, her tongue entering his mouth, as the steel under his hand seemed to soften.... Her armor seemed to be fading away, leaving his fingers dangerously close to her erect nipples. Just as he closed his thumb and forefinger upon the area he attended to attack with his mouth, the two heard the tent flap fold back.

Cursing silently, he pulled away from the intense embrace and looked at the teenage looking boy in the entrance way. What they had heard, was the flap closing behind him, Condar's mind wondered how long the insolent boy had stood there.

Underneath the messenger's hat, the boy's short black hair looked ruffled beyond repair, as boy's hair tended to do. The messenger's garb, dark tan, did not really seemed to fit the lad, but then, messenger's clothing rarely fit well anyways. It was a rotating job, as they needed light, small boys to ride atop fast steeds. Once boys got too tall or too heavy, it was time to find another. The boy, himself, was probably a bit too tall, maybe a bit too old, but the thing that was truly out of place was the boy's insolence. Normally these boys were cowed by their youth and their job, run ragged to all corners of the kingdom and beyond. But this messenger, above his opaque riding veil, had sharp piercing green eyes that looked directly into Condar's, almost as if that boy had something to prove.

The captain of Condar's guard stood back up to her full height and made sure her armor had faded back into existence, covering her flesh, before turning around to face the boy. The captain wondered if the boy had seen the vanishing armor, it would have been a shame to kill another one because they saw too much. She turned and made eye contact with the youth. The youth stared right back at her. In those green eyes, the captain saw grim determination, and an understanding….

No, the messenger was not a boy. The messenger had been a boy when he rode up, but that boy was now tied up, naked, by the latrine designated for the women guards. His discovery would cause enough of a disturbance in a few minutes that the elven woman who had stolen his clothes and used them to sneak into Condar's tent could escape. The assassin had seen enough of the guard woman's magic to know that she was not what she seemed either. Condar's guard captain was actually Condar's male mage within some form of illusion spell. The prince obviously had interesting tastes….

She went over the plan again, as she looked at the two hoping it would all work. With just a bit of revision it should. Either way, it was a plan.

Condar leaned forward in his chair and exclaimed, "Well, out with it!"

It was hard not to laugh at his prominent erection under his clothes. He really had been into that kiss, had he not? Despite the comedy of the situation, the messenger said, "Sorry, my liege, I am exhausted from the ride, I am here to tell you, the King is dead."

"WHAT?!?!" Prince Kell fell into his seat. "How is this possible?!?!"

The messenger smiled under her veil and in the same false voice, "The Bard you killed, she came back from the grave." The blood drained from the Prince's face as he looked upon those green eyes again, he knew he was in trouble, and that a trap was clamping down upon him. The assassin removed the messenger's hat and veil throwing them aside, revealing an elven face that the Prince knew all too well.

"And now, she's here for you."

Condar Kell yelled for help, but the yell went unheard. The Bard that should have been dead had already created a magical barrier of sound encompassing the tent. Part of Condar wanted to think how odd it was to see the so-called Emerald Bard in the drab messenger's garb, but he did not have the time, as she sprang directly into action.

The mage, sprang into action just as quickly. He dropped his illusion instantly. He did it to confuse his combatant, as the mage was quite a bit shorter than the female form he had just taken. What he had not realized was that the bard he had helped kill had a good memory and had dealt with illusionary forms many times. The thrown tomahawk like axe caught him directly in the face before he had fully brought up the illusion of clothes.

Blood from the thrown axe splattered everywhere. The blood fountaining from the wound made more of a scene than the mage's completely naked body, posed mid-spell with a semi-erect phallus. The blood sprayed

across the inside of the tent, the maps, and the stunned
Prince.

The bard that should have been dead walked
towards the blood spattered prince. He was so in shock
that he could not even mutter Amalric's name. That
man, the mage, had been his childhood friend, his lover,
and his confidant. Amalric was so powerful a mage that
Condar found it inconceivable Amalric could die,
especially while he still lived. But live he must.

The bard that should have been dead smiled, not a
drop of blood had landed upon her. It was like he was
watching some trick of the light, some magic spell, as the
bringer of his death walked towards him. Only when the
elven sword glinted in the candle light did Prince Condar
Kell finally spring into any form of action.

The prince fought like a madman, in a crazed
frenzy. Only when Condar reached for his ceremonial
scepter did Deeya see her lute on the carpets of the tent
by the makeshift throne. He wielded like a club. The
undead vision from his nightmares, though, parried
every move he had with amazing, artistic skill. The
metal rang inside the tent with an almost deafening
cacophony. Condar's mouth frothed as he shattered the
table that had been holding up all the maps of the area.

He looked at the elf, as he picked his make-shift
club out of the rubble and said, "You elves, living for
eternity, you have such amazing power, yet you let the
rest of the world suffer."

"So, its simple bigotry that put me in the ground?"

Prince Kell laughed, "If only.... No, you know why
you wound up in that grave."

Deeya parried a sloppy strike from Kell, using the movement of the parry to pivot, spin around, and kick the man in the jaw. This sent the man flying, only to land upon his former friend and lover with a sickening splat. A large amount of blood had oozed out of the naked man which now clung to the prince, soaking into his clothes and matting his red hair. Deeya stood above the man, with her right hand on her hips. "Oh really? And what was that reason again?"

Condar wiped his mouth as he struggled to get up, leaving a streak of gore filled blood across his face and red beard. "Because, you were impeding my progress, the progress of the nation."

The bard raised an eyebrow, as she felt more and more like herself with each passing moment. She almost scoffed before she said, "Truly? You think that Ryn'Vey was going to help you become King?"

Condar growled and swiped at the annoying not-dead bard with his nicked scepter that was missing so many jewels that it really was just a jagged club. Deeya easily stepped away from the blow. He used the momentum to get back to his feet.

Deeya set her deep green eyes upon him as he struggled to his feet.

"No, after you took away my chances to become king, by removing my father from his throne and having him killed, I realized that having my fat, stupid uncle as the king was even better than having to wait until my father died of old age. I was whispering into his ear, making him build that army. She was helping him, not me."

"Yes, the King told me that it wasn't his plan, just before I removed his head."

"Liar!" he yelled as he came for her.

Deeya blocked the attacks with ease. The man was infuriated and fighting like the madman he appeared to be. Finally, Deeya stopped parrying and simply stepped out of the way. Condar fell face first into his make shift throne, which supported the weight of his face smashing into the back of the seat.

He blinked away the pain, turned over from his rather undignified position, and sat in the chair, like a child, with his butt almost on the ground.

"You could have killed me just then, why didn't you?"

Before he realized it, that long, elegant elven blade was at his throat, and the bard's face was inches from his own. Her breath smelled like hardtack, the dried rations that soldiers eat on long marches, and blood. But then, everything smelled like blood in the tent.

She said, in a vicious, commanding voice, "Make no mistake, you will not leave this tent alive, but I have to know.... Why was I involved in this?"

"Because you knew what really happened, how this all started, with the dragon attack." A tear slid out of Condar's eye as he sighed softly. "When you returned to slay Ryn'Vey, to stop our plans...I knew you had finally returned to settle the original debt of us wronging you."

Deeya narrowed her eyes. He was finally circling the truth. "So, you tried to kill me because you thought I had come for you, to end the plans you had set in motion?"

He nodded weakly. "You had every reason to. My father started it all, which is failed ascent to the throne, and my aunt was part of the setup, though not by choice. My uncle was ignorant to it all, but I was able to whisper into his ear...."

Deeya pressed the blade more firmly against his throat. "And the army? Ryn'Vey's involvement?"

His face twisted. "To unite the country under my uncle's banner...and my friend...Amalric...." Tears flowed now from both eyes as he glanced at his dead friend. "When my uncle was unmanageable, Amalric would pose as the king...."

Deeya blinked. The illusion magic. Amalric was not only posing as Condar's guard captain...but impersonating the king himself....

"We were going to bring about a golden age, first for the country, then for the entire world...."

Deeya shook her head, it was not about becoming king, it was about ruling the entire world.... There was one detail that stood out to Deeya above all else, though. "Considering how you treated me, this *golden age* would leave no place for non-humans."

Condar pivoted under the lithe elf and punched her square across the face. Deeya spun, but did not fall, even though she was unsteady on her feet. Luckily, he did not have a gauntleted hand. Condar grasped the hilt of his scepter and stood up to his full height, towering over Deeya. "Because you eternals, you have the power to make this world a much better place, with your magics. Yet, you sit over there on your island and do nothing, while the world wars and dies. I will bring the peace and health to the world which you reject."

Deeya shook her head, which was still ringing from the punch. "You humans do nothing but kill each other in the name of a war to bring peace. You justify it with many names, your kingdoms, your surnames, commands from your made up gods, but in the end it comes down to a word you do not even understand. Power is not peace." She raised her sword to point it directly at the Prince's chest. "You don't deserve the short life you live."

Kell grinned at the female elf. His punch had landed with a bloody fist, so there was a huge smear of blood across her face. He grinned the grin of a stupid human who knew that, in the end, he would win. "Who are you, Bard? You know how to fight, and you are always in the right place at the right time to further your own agenda? Are you a spy?"

Deeya rolled her eyes yet held her sword steady. "I'm just an information gatherer. I go to places, sing, and listen. I share that information with whomever I please."

"And what information did you gather here?"

"That your mage friend assassinated the king, then came here to assassinate you, the wounds he inflicted before you caught him in the face with a blade finished his job after he perished."

Condar swung his scepter viciously at Deeya's head. She ducked and stabbed him in the chest.

"Your cousin, Gundar Kell, under the tutelage of your Aunt Sasha, will take the throne." She ducked again, and cut his sword arm. The cut was swift and deep, cutting the muscles underneath to the bone. The scepter flew out of his hand, bouncing upon the carpet floor of the tent. "And this army of yours will never be raised, and your plan will be forgotten."

Condar yelled one last battle cry and charged the bard he killed just a couple of nights ago. Deeya easily pivoted out of the way, picked up a sword from the ruin of the table, and thrust it deep within the chest of Prince Condar. The short lived, never crowned King of the Kell dynasty took two more steps before he fell over on top of the dead body of his comrade, and died on top of his lover.

Deeya stood there, her head bowed, with two dead bodies in front of her. She had work to do, before the bodies were discovered. She had to collect her lute and axe, stage the bodies better, clean her face, and sneak out.

But for now, as she stood amongst death for the umpteenth time in her life, she reflected upon all that had transpired to bring death upon this land. Needless death, stupid death. Death that she had to bring to this place to right a wrong. But Deeya's sad, emerald eyes begged the question:

Why is death the only way to answer humanity's wrongs?

Movement 3: Standing Upon an Empty Grave

A regal woman stood amongst shadows falling deep within a meadow upon a hill. She looked to be in her fifties, yet that was only the undue stress that had been put upon her in her just over forty years of life. Her long red hair was done up in a braid that reached the small of her back. Her face was creased with the pain of all she had suffered in recent months and with all that had suffered around her.

Behind her, her entourage consisted of a few Ladies-in-Waiting, a handful of guards, and a young boy who was playing with his nanny in the grass not far away. In all consideration, this should have been a scene set in a park, but the woman stood before a small hole in a raised mound of undried earth. Opposite her stood a rusty sword, stabbed into the ground with a sign on it, like a tombstone for a wayward soul.

The woman then took the flower she had been clutching to her breast and laid it upon the shallow, now empty grave. As she rose back to her full height, another person walked into the meadow, ignored by all, as if she was a ghost only the regal, red haired woman could see.

El'Mindeeya Do'Katal was resplendent in her green traveling outfit. She always kept spares, in case the one she was wearing got dirty or damaged, one of which had been ruined beyond repair. Amazingly, she looked the same as she always did, considering all that she had recently been through, a short female Forest Elf with a lute strapped to the pack on her back.

The woman eyed the elven bard as Deeya came close. Deeya looked around at the meadow and said, "This place looks different in the daytime. Tranquil almost."

The woman looked at the bard and said, "This was the mound upon which the first Kell stood, claiming the land for the future of his family."

Deeya sighed, "A rather auspicious place to have been buried."

The woman sniffed and looked at Deeya in the eyes, "Considering you saved the dynasty by destroying it…yes, auspicious is a good word." She stood watching the bard a moment longer before saying, "Why are you here?"

Deeya looked at the woman and said, "Because, Queen Mother Sasha Kell, I wanted to pay my respects to the new Kell upon the throne."

The Queen Mother sniffed again, "And why am I here?"

The bard smiled, "To remind you of what you warned me about. After your father died in that dragon attack, you warned me this country was going to rot from within, that you would be a better Queen to the

people, and raise a better King than your eldest brother.
I stood with you to make sure that brother was deposed.
Yet your younger brother won the throne. You have
your chance now, to prove to me, and your people, that
we did not make a mistake with that revolution you
started."

The Queen Mother straightened a bit. Her life had
practically turned to shit when she suggested starting the
revolution. Her brothers, though, were a pox upon the
land. Her eldest brother had been an evil, sadistic brute
that had playfully raped her in their youth. Her younger
brother was a dimwitted oaf that she had hoped to
control. But alas…her elder brother's son, Condar turned
out to be worse than his father. He latched on to the
new king first.

Sasha had never been allowed to marry, but she
had a child with her friend and lover of many years,
before he was sentenced to death for being inappropriate
with the sister of the King. Since then, she had been
almost in exile, living in a quaint country estate to the
east of the capital. Always in view of the castle, but
completely cut off from it. Luckily, though, she had her
ways to get intrigue from court, and raise her son the
way she saw fit.

Sasha was a brilliant woman, and she was smart
enough to know the unsaid threat when Deeya said the
words framing it. She quickly pointed it out by saying,
"Why does it sound like there was an 'or else' that was
left unsaid."

Deeya narrowed her eyes and squatted down next
to the grave. "If there was, I wasn't going to say it. I hate
killing, I always have. I am supposedly going to live

forever, yet surrounding me on all sides is death. I walk through a world that changes, fluctuates, and moves on." Deeya tossed a rock into the small puddle at the bottom of the hole she had dug herself out of almost a full week before. "I should have just walked away."

The Queen Mother straightened her corset as she said, "But you did not."

Deeya stood and looked at the taller woman. Deeya was older than her by sixty years but looked to be her junior by at least twenty. "No, I did not. I did not walk away then, and I did not walk away this time."

The Queen Mother then said, in a very cool tone, "But history will record that you did. I swear to you Bard: that I, and my son, will return the Kell Dynasty to its former glory, loved by the people for being what my father was."

Deeya nodded gravely. "He was a good man. I'm sorry that I didn't kill the dragon before it took your father's life."

"That was a sad day. But he stood upon the ramparts with the legions of guards with dragon slaying crossbows. He knew the dragon had to be destroyed there and then, at the castle, or it would have rampaged throughout the kingdom. He did what a King had to do, he stood against the forces that threatened his people.

Deeya stood back up and nodded, "He was a great King, a shame his eldest son warned the dragon we were coming, and set him upon the land."

Sasha nodded as well. "All three of us dealt with our father's demise in our own way. And now, after all this time, I am the one that gets to try to live up to his legacy."

"No, you have to rebuild his legacy, the people, they no longer say the name 'Kell' with love."

Sasha donned a determined smile and said, "No, but they will again. My son will grow to earn his title, as will all who follow."

Deeya stepped closer, broke protocol, and laid a hand on the Queen Mother's own hands. "Make the best of your life, and his," Deeya said, nodding at the boy.

"I shall. And...." Sasha, the Queen Mother, removed her hands from the Bard's, reached into a pocket on the bodice of her dress, and retrieved an envelope, handing it to Deeya. "This arrived for you." Deeya took the letter and inclined her head. The Queen Mother then continued, asking, "I never got to know, the artifact...."

Deeya smiled and walked away from the Queen Mother before turning and said, "The artifact that was to be my payment for the dragon?"

Sasha returned the smile and said, "Yes, the one I gave you after everything went so wrong for us."

Deeya unholstered her axe and held it up for the Queen Mother, who smiled and said, "The hilt.... Is it a magical weapon?"

Deeya smirked wryly and said, "Very much so."

The two women shared a smile, a smile that went far deeper than this small meeting. A smile that was shared by those that had conspired together for something better in the world and through more hardships than either could count, somehow succeeded.

After a few moments of them grinning at each other, Deeya slapped her letter in her hand and said,

"Thank you, Queen Mother Sasha Kell, may your reign be enlightened and blessed by your ancestors."

Sasha Kell inclined her head back, "And thank you, Emerald Bard, El'Mindeeya, may your music bring more happiness than you wish to spread."

Deeya turned and walked away. Halfway across the clearing, she opened the letter and paused. She read the lines hurriedly, then started to sing a song. Behind her, Sasha Kell looked on, as Deeya turned into a blur of motion and vanished into the trees.

--

After a few hundred yards in a handful of seconds, Deeya slowed to a walk. She read the words written by Mindee Do'Katal, her daughter. It was a long journey north, but nothing could keep her from her daughter. Not bigotry, not buried secrets, nor deadly traps.

She went over the words in her head:

> Mom,
>   We need to speak as quickly as you can make it to me. Aloucia is coming with me to Fo'Est, please meet me there. Something amazing has happened, yet as much has gone wrong. My green eyes need to see yours.
>   Hurry,
>   Mindee

She wondered what could be so urgent for Mindee to use their code: "green eyes." There was only one way to find out. By the date on the letter, it had already taken a month to find her. Another month on the road would pass before she could see Mindee again.

Deeya settled the pack that held her belongings and lute on her shoulders, thinking about the long road ahead of her. The cities she would pass would be around some of the most beautiful places that existed upon the world. Through it all, it would give her time to clear her head.

The world already held more than enough suffering, so why were so many people dedicated to spreading it further?

Deeya walked through the trees, shortcutting to the main road. Pain, sorrow, and loss still pressed against her like the weight of the wet earth she'd clawed through to rise again. Deeya had been raised away from elven kind, among humanity that had taught her long ago, that survival always demanded blood and yet she had never grown callous to it. Though it had a way of staining one's soul. She wondered if she would ever be able to clean away the blood she had been forced to spill.

This outlook had always separated her from her elven kin. She was immortal like them, which separated her from everyone else in the world.

Tonight, she felt set apart from the world at large. Tonight, she felt like a woman walking through the ruins of a world too broken to save, hoping her daughter would give her a reason to keep trying.

THE END

Keep reading for a Preview of

Ballad of the Emerald Bard
Opus 2:
The Suite of Wolves, Poison, and Revelry

A Preview of Opus 2 from The Cantata of a Quiet Venom

Movement 2: Trading Places

You can't love some-thing wild   and have it not lose it's wiles

Deeya stirred as sunlight crept across the sky, streaking it with pinks, oranges, and buttery gold. Wrapped in the thick warmth of Aloucia's wolf cloak, she lay curled against the cool morning air, her bare skin shielded by its dense fur. She rarely slept, not fully, but last night had pulled her into a deep, satisfied slumber, which refreshed her entire being. Her body still thrummed with echoes of their lovemaking; each breath tinged with memory.

The cloak around her explained the dream.

Bits of it clung to her mind like dew, hazy and strange. She remembered the dream version of Seraphas: the dark elf form with obsidian skin, kneeling, their voice desperate and raw, begging to be allowed to climax. That image should've unsettled her. But Deeya knew better. She'd long since learned that Seraphas, for all their divine control over the dream-realm, couldn't quite wrest dominance from her. Not when desire and will burned so fiercely in Deeya's soul.

The first time they met in that shadowed space, the god had tried to overpower her. Tried to make her submit. Deeya had thrown her out.

Since then, the game always played out the same. Seraphas conjured temptations, illusions, and lust, but in the end, it was always the wolf-goddess who knelt.

Deeya smiled faintly. She let the last fragments of the dream slip away as more familiar sounds reached her ears. Aloucia was humming to herself while working the fire.

She turned her head and spotted her: crouched by the flames, dressed now except for the cloak, tending breakfast with effortless grace. The half-elf's braid swung as she moved, beads glinting in the morning light. A scattering of silver studs ran up the ridges of her ears, catching the sun alongside the small green ring in her lower lip and the gleam of the nose stud above it. Even her tongue, Deeya recalled with a twitch of heat, held a hidden stud that clicked softly against her teeth when she thought. Her movements were simple and unhurried, but there was power in them; in the muscles shifting beneath her dark skin, in the steadiness of her hands, in the wild, easy confidence that lived in her body even in quiet moments like this.

Deeya watched her for a while, not as an object to be admired, but as someone beloved. The memories came unbidden, the fire of their passion, the secrets shared beneath stars, the softness of laughter tangled with moans. She remembered, too, the moment it had shifted, when she realized that Aloucia was falling for her, leashing pieces of herself to Deeya without even meaning to.

But Aloucia wasn't meant to be tethered.

Raised by a god of wolves, she would always need to run free, to chase the wind with no strings attached.

Deeya had learned to accept that. To love her enough to let her go when she needed it. Because Aloucia always came back. And in that, there was something deeper than any vow or promise.

It was enough. It was everything. It had to be.

Without warning, Aloucia turned her blue eyes towards Deeya's and smiled warmly. "I was lucky to have found you."

Deeya, snuggling deeper into the wolf cloak for warmth and chuckled, "Luck? Like you weren't using that cute nose of yours to track me."

Aloucia smile broadened as she stirred the contents of the small skillet over the fire. "I've missed you, *Laegannar*," she admitted, playfully conceding to Deeya's teasing nods to Aloucia's acute senses. "I needed help. Then I smelled you on the wind and I knew I'd found it."

Deeya sat up, wrapping the wolf cloak tighter around her shoulders. The warm still lingering on her skin had nothing to do with the fire, as she noticed Aloucia's eyes flicker briefly to the gaps created by the movement. It warmed her deeply, knowing the small flashes of bare skin were being enjoyed by her lover.

"I'm headed north," Deeya said, "Mindee sent for me."

Aloucia's stirring slowed. She and Mindee had grown close over the years; both half-elven, close in age, both shaped by lives caught between two worlds. They'd met when Deeya brought Aloucia to the University of Tran'Tar, and the bond had been instantaneous. Tattoos, piercings, quiet rebellion, and loud laughter. Somehow, Mindee had never asked about Aloucia's relationship with her mother. Or maybe she hadn't needed to. Maybe she'd seen the truth before either of them had found the words for it.

"So much has happened, I don't even know where to start," Aloucia's words tumbled out in a rush, her concern palpable. "I'm glad Mindee's letter reached you. She...she really does need you. But...." She hesitated, exhaling slowly before drawing in a steadying breath, "But my brother is in danger."

Deeya arched an eyebrow in surprise, "Brother?" she asked with a blink. "You have a brother?"

"Well...a half-brother," she corrected softly. "Deeya, he is full Elven. You remember my mother's story?" A mix of emotions crossed Aloucia's face as she looked at Deeya expectantly.

When they'd first met, Aloucia had no clue who her parents had been. She been left at an orphanage for mixed-blood children who were nameless and without roots. Later, Aloucia had uncovered the truth. Her mother, Elenya, had once been enslaved by an elven mage who trafficked in both elven and human captives. Before Aloucia was born, a dark-skinned human man, from one of the nomadic tribes of the Desert of Shae, had helped Elenya escape. Their freedom was short-lived. The mage hunted them down, murdered the man, whose sacrifice allowed Elenya to avoid being captured. She was able to stay on the run long enough to give birth to Aloucia, and leave her at the orphanage.

Years after meeting Deeya, Aloucia had found her, injured and hiding in a healer's hut, on the run again after yet another escape. Together, she and Deeya had stood with Elenya, and slain the mage who had haunted her life.

"Of course, Puppy." Deeya's voice softened with memory. "I don't think I'll ever forget helping you find your mother."

Aloucia's eyes welled with tears as Deeya spoke. Deeya leaned forward, without hesitation, the wolf cloak slipping from her shoulders as she touched Aloucia's arm.

"Being there with you for that moment was honestly one of the greatest honors of my life," Deeya said earnestly.

Aloucia's response was a tender kiss, her lips lingering on Deeya's. During the moment, Deeya's finger traced the scar on Aloucia's right cheekbone, a silent thank you shared between the long time lovers.

"Things have…changed," Aloucia said softly, leaning her forehead against Deeya's before leaning back and fixing her gaze onto Deeya's. "The mage…he's back. He found my mother. Killed her. And now he's hunting my half-brother."

Deeya confusion was palpable, "Wait…what?"

Aloucia wiped a tear away and chewed on her lip ring. "Yeah. He has some way to cheat death…."

Deeya's mouth hung open, stunned. Deeya left the shelter of the wolf cloak completely, enveloping Aloucia into a fierce embrace. "Puppy…," she whispered softly. "I'm so sorry…."

Aloucia closed her eyes and leaned into the hug, breathing in the scent of Deeya's skin, finding it soothing, familiar, and strong. When she finally pulled back, she stirred the skillet again, deliberately focusing on the task instead of Deeya's skin.

The smell of food made Deeya's stomach rumble.

"So," she said carefully, "this half-brother of yours, he's the mage's son?"

Aloucia nodded silently, her teeth worrying at her lip ring. One hand twitched toward her braid but stilled. Deeya waited, giving her space, pulling the wolf cloak back around her shoulders, but keeping it open.

Finally, Aloucia drew in a breath. "The mage saw part of some prophecy. Or maybe it was a dream. It said a female descended from him would actually be able to slay him once and for all."

Deeya's eyes narrowed. "Descended how?"

Aloucia's expression twisted. "To him, it means any woman born of his bloodline. Any child of his children." Her voice thickened with disgust as she reached for their bowls. "He's obsessed. Tracks his children. Watches them. Keeps them from having daughters."

Deeya shivered, but not from the cold. "Goddess. He's sounding more and more human the more this story goes on." She pulled the cloak tighter around her.

"He's worse than you know," Aloucia muttered. "Probably undead."

Deeya winced. "Lich?"

Aloucia gave a humorless nod, giving the stew another few stirs. "Or something like it."

"So, your brother...," Deeya prompted gently, sensing the hesitation.

"Do'Varna," Aloucia said. "I found him through my mother's last words." She exhaled slowly, her jaw tense. "And his mate...," Aloucia took in another deep breath. "His mate is pregnant."

"Then the child is a target," Deeya said, her posture stiffening.

"If Do'Grane, the mage, has found out," Aloucia said, spooning stew into Deeya's bowl, "then yes."

"Do they know if it's a girl?"

Aloucia shook her head. "Too early. She's barely showing. Hasn't started wearing loose clothes yet, so its noticeable, if you know what to look for." Aloucia sighed. "Hopefully Do'Grane doesn't. Do'Varna is keeping her hidden regardless."

The fire crackled quietly. Deeya took the offered bowl, sniffing at the rich scent of spiced squirrel meat. Deeya had set snares the night before in hopes of a breakfast, Aloucia had obviously helped herself, seasoning it with the pouch of herbs she always carried.

"I'm sure Mindee won't mind me making a small detour," Deeya said with a smirk, using her fork to take a mouthful of meat.

Aloucia began spooning soup into her own bowl. "Yeah, about that...," she said softly, blushing and trying not to chew on her lip ring again.

But the words died in her throat as Deeya lurched forward, bowl dropping from her hands.

Choking.

Deeya's face was turning blue.

"Deeya?" Aloucia dropped her own bowl and scrambled across the small space between them, hands flying to Deeya's skin. Her clammy skin....

It wasn't choking, it was something else.

Aloucia was a natural druidess and could wield the magic of nature. Enhanced by the dwarven tattoos on her body, her mother's passed on magical abilities allowed Aloucia to cast magic by pulling the life force of life around her. The grass around the campsite started withering away as Aloucia tried to probe to figure out what was wrong.

"Deeya, what's wrong?" Aloucia desperately pleaded. "I need to know so I can fix it!"

"Don't...know...," Deeya struggled to say, gasping, barely able to form words. "Ripping...cold...."

Aloucia pressed a hand to Deeya's forehead, another to her chest, and began chanting. Tattoos flared with shimmering silver power as life energy rippled from her into the bard's collapsing form. The circle of dead grass expanded outward from them.

Come on...tell me what's wrong! Aloucia's inner voice echoed in her head. *I can't fix it if I don't know.* The silence that echoed in her mind was disconcerting. But she couldn't waste time trying to guess why the wolf goddess was quiet.

Deeya convulsed, a sharp shudder rippling through her limbs.

Aloucia dove deeper, pushing her spirit through the threads of Deeya's being, searching frantically with growing desperation...until, at last, she found it.

The cold icy tendrils of the poison.

But it wasn't just a toxin. There was something else laced into it, something that felt...alive.

A spell....

It was coiled and cold, with intent behind it. It wasn't merely poisoning Deeya. It was *unraveling* her.

Unspooling the soul's tether from the body. Peeling it away like thread from flesh.

Aloucia's eyes snapped open.

She surged to her feet and kicked the skillet off the fire. It crashed into the dirt, scattering stew across stone and sand. The scent of burnt herbs clung to the air.

"Okay.... Think. Think." Her breath came ragged. "Purge first. Yes. Purge, then...."

She turned, only to find Deeya already doubled over, retching violently.

"No..., Deeya. Lie down," Aloucia implored. "I have a plan...."

END OF PREVIEW

Continue in Opus 2: The Suite of Wolves, Poison, and Revelry

About the Author

Dan Bonser was born in 1976 in Bangs, Texas. The first books that ever truly captivated him was The Sword of Truth by Terry Goodkind and the entire Wheel of Time series by Robert Jordan. After he escaped Texas in his early twenties, he lived for 11 years in North Carolina. There he learned what it truly meant to be in love and at peace with the world. There he found the works of authors such as Robert Jordan, Jacqueline Carey, and Laura K. Hamilton. Even though he had been writing for years at this point, and known he wanted to be a writer, it was at this point he realized the true scope of what he wanted to write.

Married to his amazing, and already published, wife Lisa, in his late thirties, and after several failed attempts to join the middle class he has started college again (for the second time). Writing, which had been a progressive hobby, became his release during times of stress and happiness. With new found joy he began writing The Ballad of the Emerald Bard for his blog, and though the blog had only limited success he was inspired to truly push out something he could be proud of.

Dan has been writing with imaginative flair since the early 1980s, and he has never stopped. From poetry to his love of fantasy, Dan will continue to write until he absolutely can no longer share his dreams and visions with the world.

You can find his blog at http://abrainlessnod.blogspot.com
His photography page at http://www.emeraldreflection.com
You can find him on social media by way of Facebook and Twitter

A Note On Editions

Most edition changes have been purely proofreading, as with all large amounts of text, a few errors slipped through and have been corrected when caught. For the update to third edition, I also changed some of the formatting, which include the artwork by Tarah Hardy, as she made the beautiful blade of the Sonnetic Axe, which is now display at the front of each story. Formatting includes spacing, margins, headers, and other small fixes to make the book more enjoyable. I left the "About the Author" section alone, as it is a snapshot of the time the book was published.

Starting with fourth edition, I worked through the text with fresh, older eyes, removing a problematic issue which has plagued the book since its inception. I fully believe that, as of now, the experience for everyone will be far more enjoyable, and its far closer to my original intention than it was when I first published it.

This fifth (and hopefully) final edition does one final grammar pass, along with the addition of a preview of Opus 2.

www.ingramcontent.com/pod-product-compliance
Lightning Source LLC
Chambersburg PA
CBHW020418110726
47899CB00006B/2044